DARED
and
Kissed

THE SCOTSMAN'S YULETIDE BRIDE

BY
BREE WOLF

This is a work of fiction. Names, characters, businesses, places, brands, media, events and incidents are either the products of the author's imagination or used in a fictitious manner.

Any resemblance to actual persons, living or dead, or actual events is purely coincidental.

DARED

and

Kissed

THE SCOTSMAN'S YULETIDE BRIDE

Prologue

Seann Dachaigh Tower, Scottish Highlands, December 1801

Seven Years Earlier

Drawing her cloak tighter around her to ward off the chill of the crisp winter morning, sixteen-year-old Emma Stewart of Clan MacDrummond stood on the edge of the clearing, half-hidden behind a large boulder, her deep brown eyes drawn to the young men as they crossed their swords in training.

Their faces shone rosy in the cool winter's air as they moved back and forth, the metal of their blades gleaming in the faint morning sun. Emma could feel the clash of their swords resonate in her bones as it echoed through the stillness of the small glen. A cold shiver ran down her spine, and she breathed a sigh of relief that war had come and gone long ago.

These were times of peace, and the young men of her clan were merely training to keep a sharp mind and humble heart as their laird demanded of them. He was a good and kind man and had seen their clan through many trials. Still, his health was failing, and soon his son, Cormag, would follow in his footsteps and become Laird.

Shifting her gaze to the tall dark-haired man, Emma marvelled at the stillness with which he moved. There was no exertion on his face, and here and there, it seemed as though his feet barely touched the ground. He was a strange man, the laird's son, taciturn and reticent in many ways, and yet, watchful and observant, his grey eyes sharp like those of a hawk.

Emma wondered what he saw when he looked at her, and another shiver went down her back. Quickly, she turned her gaze to the other young men, fair-haired Ian and dark-haired Garrett. However, it was the sight of Finnegan MacDrummond that made her heart leap into her throat.

At least six years her senior, Finn stood tall, his shoulders squared as he watched Ian's approach, his sparkling green eyes narrowed as he prepared for his opponent's attack. Their swords clashed, and Emma held her breath.

Laughter echoed to her ears as Finn drew back, running his hand through his dark auburn curls. "Ye fight like a wee bairn, Ian! Is this all ye've got?"

Determination and a good deal of humour rested on Ian's face as he charged toward his friend, their swords colliding once again, sending sparks flying through the soft fog still lingering this early in the morning.

Transfixed, Emma watched as the men continued their training, her eyes locked on the young man who had stolen her heart so long ago. She could not recall a time when the mere sight of him had not stolen her breath and addled her mind. He was sweet and kind, and his green eyes always sparkled with exuberance and a hint of mischief. He stood by his friends and always lent a helping hand to those who needed it. He loved this land, their home, fiercely, and yet, every now and then she could see a yearning for adventure in his eyes, to see the world and know more than the small circle of life into which he had been born.

Oh, Emma knew him well, and yet, they had never truly spoken to one another. Nothing beyond a few meaningless courtesies here and there. Emma wondered if he even knew her name.

A faint giggle drifted to her ears from the tree line in her back, jarring Emma back to the here and now. Glancing over her shoulder, she spotted Aileen and Sorcha standing half-hidden behind a large oak, their eyes glowing as they whispered to one another.

Sighing, Emma squared her shoulders, reminding herself why she was here, why she had risen so early and trudged through the woods, her hem now soaked with morning dew.

"Go," Aileen hissed from behind the tree, keeping her voice low, her eyes darting to the young men, a touch of apprehension in them as she feared that they might have taken notice.

The young men, however, were so engrossed in their training that not one of them looked up and spotted the girls standing not too far off, watching them with rapt attention.

Emma nodded, then turned back, her eyes once more drifting to Finn, her target. Instantly, her heart sped up, and panic flooded her being. Was she mad to have come here? To have agreed to their game?

Her fingers curled into her palms, and her muscles tensed as though urging her back. No, she would not turn and run. Lifting her head, Emma squared her shoulders. This was her chance-her only chance-and she would take it. After all, it was only a dare, and if Finn rejected her then at least she could laugh it off and pretend that none of it affected her in any way. All she had to do was keep a straight face and not let him see how much she cared for him.

Inhaling a deep breath, Emma stepped out from behind the boulder, momentarily grateful for the shrubbery that still hid her from their sight. Nevertheless, soon she would have to reveal herself and it was still a good distance from the edge of the clearing to where they stood with their swords crossed. Would they address her? Would they ask what she was doing here? If so, what would she say?

"Ye're a fool," Emma whispered to herself as she took another step forward. "They'll laugh at ye, and yer cheeks will turn bright red."

The moment Emma stepped around the last of the shrubbery, she froze as she found Cormag looking straight at her, his sharp, hawk-like eyes colliding with hers. The hint of a frown touched his brows, and she wondered how long he had known of her presence. Had he truly spotted her just now? Or had he somehow...known as he often seemed to know things he should not know?

"Go," Aileen hissed once more, and as though Emma's feet had a life of their own, they complied. Goose bumps rose on her arms and legs as Emma found herself walking into the clearing, her heart beating painfully in her chest as she fought down the panic that threatened to engulf her. What on earth was she doing?

The moment Cormag had stopped, turning his head to look at her, his friends had ceased their training as well. At first, confusion had come to their faces before they followed his line of sight.

Now, four sets of eyes were trained on her as Emma walked into the clearing, slowly closing the distance between them. She did her best to hold her chin high and maintain a friendly, but unaffected smile on her face. However, deep down, Emma had serious doubts that she appeared as anything else but the bundle of nerves she was. Perhaps she ought to turn and run after all!

As she drew closer, she could see their chests rising and falling with each laboured breath, the muscles in their sword arms quivering with the sudden rest. Her eyes drifted from one man to the next and then back as she willed herself not to stare at Finn lest he be able to read the intention on her face. If he did, would *he* turn and run?

Cormag's eyes narrowed in a rather unsettling way as he continued to watch her. Then he took a step back, a hint of surprise coming to his eyes as he turned to look at Finn.

Emma froze. Did *he* know?

"What are ye doing here, lass?" Garrett asked as he stepped toward her, a kind smile on his face. "Ye're not lost, are ye?"

Strangely enough, Emma managed a rather natural smile. "No, I'm not lost," she replied, a slight chuckle accompanying her words as though she truly did not have a care in the world. Surprised by this unexpected ability to mask her feelings, Emma decided to seize the moment.

Stepping around Garrett, she did her best to ignore Ian's inquisitive stare as well as Cormag's speculative gaze and kept her eyes on Finn. His green gaze narrowed slightly as he watched her approach. Still, he did not try to step away, did not address her, did not stop her in any way.

It was all the encouragement Emma needed.

Two more steps brought her to him, and she could feel the

warmth that radiated off him against her skin. His green eyes held hers, and for the barest of moments, Emma thought to see something flare to life in them. Something she had never seen there before.

But Emma did not dare linger and contemplate what it was. No, she needed to move fast, or she would miss her chance.

Without a moment's hesitation, she reached up, pushing herself up onto her toes, and pulled him down into a kiss.

The moment Finn had glimpsed her standing across the clearing, his heart had slammed to a rather unexpected halt. Her mahogany curls had danced on the soft breeze, gently brushing against her rosy cheeks and giving her the appearance of a sprite risen from the earth. She stood tall and fierce, and yet, as she had approached, the dark brown of her eyes had spoken of a vulnerable heart.

Although her gaze had travelled from one of his friends to the next, somehow Finn had known that in that moment she had come for him. The moment their eyes had met, Finn had been unable to speak, to think, to do anything but stare at her.

He could not even recall her name-if indeed he had ever known it-and yet he was certain that he would never again forget who she was.

The closer she had stepped, the more his heart had felt as though it wished to jump from his chest.

And then her lips had found his.

Dimly, Finn found himself wondering if he had strayed into a dream as he felt the softness of her lips against his own and the tentative brush of her fingers against the back of his neck, uncertain and yet daring. Her body leaned into his, and for a long moment, nothing and no one else existed but them.

And then she was gone.

From one moment to the next, her touch vanished, and Finn's eyes flew open.

As her feet carried her away from him, a teasing grin rested on her face, and yet, her eyes held no humour, but something deep and vulnerable. However, before Finn could stop her, she spun on her heel and raced across the clearing.

Chuckles rose around him, and Finn blinked as Ian and Garrett approached, large grins on their faces as they looked back and forth between him and the receding figure racing toward the tree line. "I take it ye know her," Ian remarked with a teasing grin. "Ye could've introduced us. What's the lass' name?"

Inhaling a deep breath, Finn shook his head. "I dunno know."

Gawking at him, Ian laughed, "Ye dunno know? Are ye saying a lassie ye dunno even know walks up to ye and kisses ye square on the mouth? Does this happen to ye a lot?"

More laughter followed, and Finn cleared his throat, trying his best to sort through his thoughts. "No, it doesna happen a lot," he snapped, glaring at his friend. "I assure ye I'm as surprised as ye are."

"But ye like her, do ye not?" Garrett observed as he crossed his arms in front of him, a challenge lighting up his eyes. "I've never seen ye so lost for words."

Finn swallowed, shaking his head. "She's...she's something." A smile tugged on the corners of his mouth, and he chuckled. "I've seen her around, certainly, but I've never..."

"Noticed her," Cormag supplied in his usual way as though he knew precisely what the others were thinking.

Finn nodded. "Aye."

"But ye noticed her now, aye?" Ian teased some more. "I can see that she's made quite an impression. Why don't ye go after her?"

Finn's head snapped up, and for a moment, all he could do was stare at his friend.

Shaking his head, Ian laughed, then clasped a hand on Finn's shoulder. "Go and ask her name before she kisses another."

With a bit of a shove in the right direction, Finn turned toward the tree line where she had disappeared. At first his steps were measured, but before long, large strides carried him onward. His heart once more began to dance the way it had when he had felt her lips upon his own, and he wondered how he could have failed to notice her before.

Certainly, she was young, having only recently grown into a woman, but those eyes...dark and deep like a loch full of hidden treasures, and yet, warm and delicate as though a wrong word could break her heart.

Striding past the large boulder on the edge of the glen, Finn scanned the tree line, his eyes narrowing as he tried to spot any sign of her. He glimpsed her footprints in the lush, frost-covered grass a moment before soft voices drifted to his ears.

Inhaling a deep breath as his heart once again leapt into his throat, Finn stepped forward, finding his way through the dense forest, his ears guiding him, picking out more than one voice. Silently, he slipped closer until he spotted a fair-haired head bobbing up from behind a thorny thicket growing around a group of conifers.

The young woman laughed, "I thought I would faint when I saw ye kiss him," she gasped, a hand pressed to her chest. "Was it wonderful?"

Finn frowned as he edged forward, his eyes at last falling on the dark-eyed enigma who had stolen his breath. She stood with two other, equally young women-both of whom looked familiar, but whose names Finn could not recall, either. Her face looked tense as she glanced over her shoulder toward the glen. "Let us return to the tower," she whispered, a hint of apprehension in her voice as she tried to pull the fair-haired girl onward. "I'm...chilled."

"Come now, tell us of yer conquest," the other dark-haired girl urged, an eager smile on her face. "After all, ye won the dare and proved us wrong. I never would've thought that ye'd have the courage to walk up to Finnegan MacDrummond and steal a kiss."

Finn's stomach clenched as the girl's words sank in. A dare? She had kissed him because of a dare? Nothing more?

"Tell us, did it feel wonderful?" the fair-haired girl pressed, a sigh escaping her lips. "I think I would've gone weak in the knees if it had been me."

Turning her head away, Finn's brown-eyed enigma brushed a curl behind her ear. "'Twas a kiss," she all but bit out, and the harshness cut right through Finn's tentative hopes. "Nothing more, nothing less. I won. That's all that matters." Rubbing her hands together, she beckoned the other two girls onward. "Now, let's go or I swear my toes shall freeze off."

Long after they had gone, Finn still stood leaning against the conifer at his back, his eyes closed as he replayed their words in his head. It had been nothing but a dare, and he had been a fool to think more of it. To think that there had been something between them, a silent bond that had brought them to this place the way his father had often spoken of the day he had first laid eyes on Finn's mother.

As a child, Finn had often listened to his father tell this story, his words ringing with promise that one day Finn would find the same, a woman who was his other half, a woman he would recognise instantly, who would steal his breath and claim his heart.

And for a short moment, Finn had thought to have found her...and it had stunned him into speechlessness.

If only he had known from the beginning that their encounter had meant nothing to her. Nothing more but a claimed prize. A victory. A dare won.

Cursing under his breath, Finn spun on his heel and before he knew it his fists collided with the trunk of the conifer. Pain shot up his arm and into his shoulder, and blood welled up from the scrapes on his knuckles where the hard bark had cut through his skin.

Still, the pain in his heart far exceeded any physical discomfort he felt. How dare she kiss him? Before today, he had been happily oblivious to her. He had barely even noticed her. He had been content and at peace.

And now?

Now, he was achingly aware of her. He could still feel her soft touch as though she was right in front of him, and whenever he closed his eyes, he found her dark-brown ones looking into his. What had she done to him?

Would he ever be free of her? Or would he be doomed to carry her with him for the rest of his life?

Anger filled his heart, and Finn knew that he was no longer the same man he had been upon waking that morning.

Everything had changed.

He had changed.

And there was no going back.

How dare she?

Chapter One

ANOTHER YULETIDE SEASON

Seann Dachaigh Tower, Scottish Highlands, December 1808

Seven Years Later

"Run wee fishies!" Emma called as she chased after five-year-old Niall and his three-year-old sister Blair. "Run or the auld crab will catch ye! Snap! Snap!" Opening her arms wide, she brought her palms together with a loud clap right beside the little girl's ear.

Blair shrieked in delight and doubled her efforts to evade Emma's grasp, her little legs carrying her faster and faster until she reached the other side of the great hall of Seann Dachaigh Tower. Hiding under a large table set up for the yuletide festivities, Niall waved to his sister, beckoning her forward. The moment she fell to her knees and slid under the heavy wooden table, he pulled the end of the table cloth down, hiding them both from sight.

Emma pulled to a halt. "Aw, where did my fishies go?" she pouted, hearing the children giggle from under the table. "I guess I'll have to go to bed without supper this evening." Hanging her shoulders, Emma turned and walked back to the arched doorway she and Maggie had been working on before this impromptu chase.

Shaking her head at her children, Maggie laughed, her nimble fingers attaching yet another red bow to the evergreen branch decorating the doorway. "Those little rascals," she said, a mother's delight clear in her voice. "Always up to no good." Then her blue eyes turned to Emma. "And ye are no better. Encouraging them like that." Again, Maggie shook her head, and yet, the smile on her face spoke of neither reproach nor disapproval.

Emma laughed in return, feeling her heart grow lighter.

With both her parents passed on and no family of her own, the yuletide season always made Emma wistful and brought a deep ache to her heart, a longing for warmth and comfort, love and family.

As though to mock her, Finn walked into the hall in that moment, his tall stature drawing not only her eyes as he spoke to Cormag, now laird of Clan MacDrummond after his father's passing three years ago. They spoke in hushed tones, and Emma felt her heart torn between pain and delight as it always was when her eyes caught sight of him. Although she had tried her utmost to forget about him, to silence the longing that lived in her heart, it refused to listen, yearning for a man who only ever glared at her.

Ever since that morning out in the glen when Emma had dared to steal a kiss as a young lass, everything had changed. Before, Finn had merely looked past her, his eyes barely seeing the young girl who noticed him the moment he walked into a room. After that day, he had begun to see her as well. Only, his green gaze had held nothing friendly or kind, but only disdain and a deep-seated anger that Emma could not understand. Had her kiss truly offended him that much?

And then he had left.

Over the past seven years, Finn had spent months at a time with Clan MacKinnear-again and again-and although Emma could not truly believe that she had been the one to chase him away, she could not help but feel as though he had left in order to avoid her.

Her heart ached at the mere thought of it.

"Why don't ye speak to him?"

Jarred from her thoughts, Emma turned to look at her friend, finding Maggie's gentle blue eyes watching her carefully. "I dunno know what ye mean," Emma replied before clearing her throat. Then she reached for another bow, thus turning her attention to something safer.

Maggie chuckled, her dainty feet carrying her to Emma's side as though they barely touched the ground. "Dunno pretend with me," she whispered quietly. "I promised I willna share what ye told me with anyone, but neither can I pretend that I dunno know."

Emma sighed, a part of her regretting that she had shared the events of that fateful morning with Maggie. Still, another part was glad to have found a friend she could confide in without fear that her inner-most thoughts and feelings would be passed on throughout the castle. Maggie had indeed proved herself to be trustworthy and kind-hearted...and plain-speaking as well. Emma would forever be grateful for the day her friend had come to Seann Dachaigh Tower.

"There's nothing to say," Emma mumbled under her breath, the little hairs in the back of her neck telling her that Finn had not yet left the hall. How was it that she could all but feel his presence? Why would the Fates not allow her to forget about him? Was there anything more cruel than unrequited love?

Although Emma had spent a great deal of time on convincing herself that she did in fact not care for Finn MacDrummond, her obsession with him had eventually forced her to admit that she had been fooling herself. Unfortunately, that realisation had not helped in the least. If anything at all, it had served to seal her fate. Without any sway over her own heart, she would be forever doomed to yearn for a man who hated her.

"That's not true," Maggie objected in her usual direct way. "There's quite a lot to be said. Ye will never receive an answer if ye're too scared to ask questions."

Turning to face her friend, Emma huffed, "Ye canna truly think it a good idea for me to simply walk up to him and ask why he hates me so?"

A teasing grin claimed Maggie's face. "Ye once walked up to him and stole a kiss, why not ask a simple question?"

Heat shot into Emma's face, and she could not help but glance in Finn's direction.

He and Cormag had obviously finished their conversation and were now striding toward the back exit, which led out into the courtyard. They passed by the two women, and the moment Finn's gaze veered to the side, Emma sucked in a sharp breath.

Their eyes met, and for a heart-breaking moment, the world seemed to stop in its tracks. The green in his gaze flared to life, and Emma felt the heat all the way to her toes. Still, the scowl remained on his face, telling her only too clearly what he thought of her.

Bowing her head, Emma turned away, relieved when the little hairs in the back of her neck finally calmed.

"Clearly, he affects ye as he always has," Maggie observed rather inconveniently, "and I do believe there's a reason why he would glare at ye so. Indifference doesna cause such hatred." Shaking her head, Maggie held Emma's gaze. "Nah, mind my words. There's a reason for the way he looks at ye, and ye will never know it if ye dunno speak to him."

Emma's heart skipped a beat happily, new hope surging to the surface before she forced it back down with an iron will. "Even if ye're right, it willna change what is. He doesna care for me, and I'd do well to accept that. Perhaps then I'll be able to begin a life of my own." Her gaze drifted to where Niall and Blair were playing with the castle's hounds. A sigh escaped her, and a different longing came to her heart.

"Ye will be a mother," Maggie whispered beside her, "but it will dampen yer happiness if ye choose the wrong father. Believe me."

Emma's brows drew down as she turned to look at her friend.

Always cheerful and laughing, Maggie often seemed like a force of nature despite her small stature and slender figure. She seemed one with the ground she walked on, at peace and calm, like someone born of this earth. With a gentle hand, she guided her children through life, giving them the freedom they needed to discover who they were but always holding a protective hand over their heads when needed. Whatever Maggie did, she did with a calm confidence that had always inspired awe in Emma.

And yet, her friend was not truly happy, was she?

"No marriage is perfect," Maggie continued, the slight tension in her jaw telling Emma that she was well aware of her friend's scrutiny. "Even a great love can be lost, just as a match of convenience can turn into something far deeper." She sighed and finally met Emma's gaze. "There's no telling what the future will bring. All we can do is our best and be honest with ourselves. Sometimes we make a wrong decision. It happens." Her blue eyes wide, Maggie stepped forward and grasped Emma's hands. "But sometimes a wrong decision can be avoided. Believe me, there's nothing worse...than regret."

Staring into Maggie's eyes, seeing the slight mist that clung to her lashes, Emma swallowed, realising for the first time how deeply unhappy Maggie was in her marriage. "Is Ian-?"

Clearing her throat, Maggie suddenly stepped back. "Ian is a good man and a good father," she rushed to say before Emma could ask a question that might unhinge the balance of the life she had made for herself at Seann Dachaigh Tower.

But not a good husband, Emma added in her mind. *At least not the one yer heart wants.*

Although Emma would have wanted nothing more than to ask about the mysterious man who had stolen Maggie's heart at some point in her life, she did not for the look in her friend's eyes told her how affected her heart still was. Emma knew exactly how it felt to yearn for a man for years and never have one's heart see reason and abandon its quest.

"Ye at least," Maggie suddenly said, "can still choose. Once ye have, there is no going back." A desperate plea rested in Maggie's blue eyes.

Emma sighed, not wishing to hurt her friend. "I know what ye say is true, but 'tis not only my choice. What I want doesna matter if he doesna also want the same."

"But ye dunno know what he wants unless ye speak to him."

Emma scoffed as the exhaustion of years wasted slowly caught up with her. "I dunno know? Truly? Ye've seen the way he glares at me, and ye truly think that there's a chance." Emma shook her head, knowing only too well the pain false hope could bring. "No, it'll be better for me to forget about him and...seek happiness elsewhere."

"Elsewhere?" Maggie asked, her eyes narrowing in suspicion. "Ye mean Vaughn?"

Emma tensed. "How-?"

"I've seen the way he looks at ye," Maggie interrupted, the look in her eyes still one of disapproval. "He's a good man, decent and kind and respectful, but he's not the man for ye."

"Why?" Emma frowned. "Do I not deserve such a man?"

"Of course, ye do." Sighing, Maggie reached out to grasp Emma's hand once more, the look in her eyes one of motherly indulgence, as though Emma was an unruly child unwilling to see reason. "But he deserves more."

Snatching back her hand, Emma stared at her friend. "D'ye not think me good enough for him?"

Maggie chuckled, "Dunno act like a child. I meant no such thing and ye know it. But d'ye not agree that Vaughn deserves a wife who can love him? Does he not deserve a wife whose heart doesna belong to another man?"

Sobering, Emma felt her shoulders slump as one by one every path led her to nothing but heartbreak. "Aye," she finally said. "He does deserve that." Swallowing, she looked up at Maggie. "But perhaps over time, he will conquer my heart. Perhaps..."

The look in Maggie's eyes clearly stated that she disagreed. "Ye must do what ye think right. I canna make that decision for ye. All I can do is ask ye to think about the consequences of yer decision. Think wisely for the day may come that ye wish ye had."

Emma nodded, knowing that Maggie was right. Still, every once in a while, Emma wished she could throw caution to the wind and act on impulse alone...simply to have it over with. For years now, she'd been wracking her mind, her heart, every fibre of her being about what to do and what path to choose, and she was still as torn as she had been years earlier. Would the rest of her life look like this? Trapped between what her heart desired and what her mind deemed right? Would these two never walk hand in hand?

"Speak to him," Maggie urged once more. "What do ye have to lose?"

Closing her eyes, Emma drew in a shaking breath. Indeed, what did she have to lose? Her heart? Her mind? Her sanity? If Finn rejected her outright, if he laughed in her face, if he told her she was the most awful woman he had ever met, would she be able to recover? Would she ever be happy again?

Are ye now? An annoyingly familiar voice whispered in the back of her head. A voice that sounded suspiciously like a well-meaning but rather opinionated friend.

"Ye say he hates ye," Maggie continued, her voice kind and yet insistent, "that he nothing but glares at ye."

Emma nodded, wondering what her friend was trying to tell her.

A soft smile came to Maggie's lips. "Has there never been a moment-a single moment-when he didna glare at ye? When there was something else in his eyes?"

Emma was about to shake her head when a distant memory surfaced. A memory that always brought pain and joy as though one could not exist without the other.

After Emma's mother had died giving birth to her, she had been the light of her father's life...and he had been hers. Although she had always longed for the mother she had never known, her father had been all any child could ever have hoped for. He had been an enthusiastic playmate, a passionate storyteller and a devoted protector. He had been everything to her, the sun that warmed her face and the air she breathed.

Until the day he had passed on.

Suddenly and unexpectedly.

Without warning.

One moment they had shared the midday meal, and the next he had dropped to the ground.

Emma dimly remembered the haze that had claimed her the moment she had understood that her father was lost to her. For days, she had walked the castle grounds like a ghost haunting the living. Neither tear nor smile had come to her face until the day they had buried him.

Stone-faced, she had stood by his grave, unaware of the world around her as her heart had slowly reawakened and the pain had claimed her whole. Turning away, Emma had walked and walked, leaving Seann Dachaigh Tower and its people behind her. Tears had streamed down her face, and yet, she had walked on until she had come upon a small loch.

At its banks, Emma had sunk down into the lush grass, her legs no longer able to carry her. There, she had finally succumbed to her tears, weeping for the only parent she had ever known. Painful sobs had wracked her body, shaking her limbs and breaking her into a thousand small pieces...never to be whole again.

And then all of a sudden, as though he had appeared out of thin air, Finn had been there.

Emma hadn't even known that he had returned from his latest stay with Clan MacKinnear. She had not seen him in a long time, and yet, when she had needed him...he had been there. As though the Fates had returned him to her.

Quietly, Finn had sat down beside her and pulled her into his arms, holding her tightly and letting her cry. She had buried her face in his shoulder, clinging to him like someone drowning.

As though nothing had happened, as though this had been a day like any other, the sun had commenced on its daily journey across the sky, and all the while, they had sat on the bank of the loch, his arms wrapped around her.

Not a single word had passed Finn's lips that day.

Not one.

And yet, he had sat in the grass for hours, holding her in his arms, his fingers gentle as they brushed damp curls from her temple and behind her ear. The hint of a warm smile had been on his lips that day, kind and comforting, and the green in his eyes had held nothing but compassion and understanding and perhaps-perhaps-the promise that one day the pain would not be as crushing as it had been in that moment.

When her sobs had lessened, Finn had helped her to her feet and walked her home, his arm tightly around her and her head still resting against his shoulder. He had taken her to the small cottage she had shared with her father, assisting her inside until she had dropped into her bed, exhausted in heart and body. Dimly, she remembered him draping a blanket over her. Then he had sat down on a chair in the corner, watching over her as she had drifted off to sleep.

In the morning, Finn had been gone, and Maggie had sat at her bed, her gentle ways urging Emma to hold on to her father's memory but to return to the living and reclaim her smile.

A part of Emma still wondered if the day by the loch had been a dream and nothing more. For when she next saw Finn, the look in his eyes once again held the same disappointment and anger she had glimpsed there every day since the morning in the glen when she had stolen a kiss.

And then he had left yet again.

Chapter Two

A CLAN'S TRADITION

W alking beside the cart, Finn almost bumped into Ian's
back when he suddenly drew to a halt.

"What's the matter?" Ian asked as he turned to frown at
his friend. "Are ye asleep on yer feet? 'Tis not a good day to be
absent-minded. There's work to be done."

Mumbling an apology, Finn did his best to ignore the way Ian shook
his head at him or Cormag watched him out of the corner of his eye as
though he were a rare specimen of some kind that ought to be studied.
Only Garrett seemed as absent-minded as Finn himself. Their eyes
distant, they each reached for one of the logs piled high on the horse-
drawn cart. Then they walked up to the small cottages lining the road
through the little village just outside the walls of Seann Dachaigh Tower
and handed them to the families living there as a yuletide offering. For as
long as Finn could remember, it had been a tradition for the young men
of Clan MacDrummond to cut logs prior to the festivities and then offer
them to the families of their clan, a promise that they were not alone,
that they all stood as one and would forever look out for each other.

Always had this tradition had a special meaning for Finn. After his
father had passed as well, he had felt alone, thinking himself without

family to care for him, to see when he hurt, when he was in pain, to take notice of him.

Until the day when Cormag and his friends had stopped by his parents' cottage to offer him a log and then urge him to accompany them on their way. Reluctantly, Finn had joined in and soon realised that he had not gone as unnoticed as he had feared.

"The situation with the runaways has been resolved," Garrett said, his gaze intent on Cormag as he spoke. "All I could have done I did. There is no reason for me to remain here."

Looking up, Finn found a look of great urgency on Garret's face, his shoulders tense as he handed another log to Ian, who rolled his eyes as he overheard their conversation and then trudged up to the next cottage on the road. Garrett, however, failed to notice his friend's annoyance as his attention was solely focused on their laird.

Narrowing his gaze, Cormag looked at him as he often did before he replied, a rather annoying calm resting on his features as though no emotions stirred under his skin. "I assure ye I understand yer desire to be off, and I dunno object to yer returning to England. However, I suggest ye allow reason to govern ye and hold off until the roads are safer for travel." He glanced around them at the heaps of snow blocking every path leading to and from Seann Dachaigh Tower. Even the short distance down into the village with the heavy cart had taken most of the morning. "Ye willna find yer wife any faster if ye freeze on the road."

Garrett's shoulders slumped, and yet, there was a hint of a smirk on his face at Cormag's rather rare attempt at a joke. "Aye, ye're right," he conceded, reaching for another log as Ian came trudging back. "But I canna deny that I long to be off. After all, I havena seen my wife in months."

Moaning, Ian shook his head. "Am I the only one working today?" he complained, his face dark as he all but glared at Garrett. "And ye're a fool for going after her. Ye married her after a drunken night at a tavern." Ian scoffed in contempt. "If she had truly wanted to remain yer wife, she wouldna have run off."

Garrett's face darkened at his friend's accusations. "She didna run off," he snapped as they stood almost face to face like stags about to charge. "Her brother came for her and took her back home."

"Why?" Ian huffed. "She's yer wife. Or perhaps she doesna want to be, have ye ever thought of that?"

"Enough." Cormag's calm but commanding voice cut off any further remarks as he stepped forward, his boots crunching on the snow as he moved like a giant among dwarfs. His grey eyes shifted from Garrett to Ian before he spoke again. "Garrett, ye're free to leave as soon as the roads are safe to travel." Then his gaze turned to Ian and something silent passed between the two men. A moment later, Ian drew in a heavy breath and turned back to the cart, picking up another log before he once more headed down the road.

Silence fell over their little group as they continued on, slowly working their way down the road, visiting each house and sharing a few kind words with people they had known one way or another all their lives. Still, dark looks were exchanged between Ian and Garrett, and Finn wondered why his friend was so upset with Garrett's desire to return to England and look for his wife. Their story had in fact proved quite popular among their clan.

Sent after two runaways, Garrett, Ian and Finn had travelled to Gretna Green and then split up to locate the youngsters. While Ian and Finn had searched high and low, Garrett had unexpectedly stumbled upon an English lass at the inn's tavern. Finding himself head over heels in love, Garrett had married her right then and there, taking advantage of the presence of an anvil priest that night at the inn. Upon morning, he had left his sleeping wife to seek out Ian and Finn, who had in the meantime located the runaways. Finn remembered well the guilt that had stood on Garrett's face as he had apologised for abandoning them in their quest. Still, his face had been aglow, and Finn had seen with one glance that he was in love.

Happy for his friend, Finn had congratulated Garrett and urged him to introduce them to his new bride. Garrett had been more than eager to do so. However, upon returning to their room, he had found her gone with no note to explain her whereabouts. Only from the innkeeper, they had learnt that her brother, an English lord, had come to Gretna Green and taken her back to England.

As far as Finn knew, the young lady had run off to Gretna Green with another, intending to marry him. Somehow, however, that marriage had not come to be and then her path had crossed Garrett's.

Glancing at his friend, Finn wondered if Garrett was worried that his new bride's family was less than happy to learn of their new connections and understood well his desire to be off and go after her.

Only Ian seemed less than sympathetic with Garrett's current situation.

"Where will ye go?" Finn asked, handing a log to Garrett before picking one up himself. "Where will ye start looking for her?"

Garrett shrugged. "I dunno know where her family's estate is, but Cormag suggested I speak to Lord Tynham, Maggie's brother. He might be able to help, perhaps even know her family."

Finn nodded before they split ways and each knocked on another door. He had all but forgotten that Ian's wife, Maggie, had grown up in England, the daughter of an English lord, who had passed away a few years back, leaving his title and estate to Maggie's older brother. After all, considering Maggie's speech and mannerism, it was only too easy not to see her as an English lady but as a Scottish lass. Soon after her arrival at Seann Dachaigh Tower, home of her mother's clan, the Highlands had stolen her heart and turned her into a true Scot.

In the beginning, Finn had wondered if it had been Ian's doing. If it had been their love that had made her feel at home in the Highlands in such a profound way. However, lately, Finn had begun to have doubts.

Truth be told, Ian looked far from happy these days. His comments with regard to Garrett's situation proved that all the more.

"Perhaps I should go with ye," Finn heard himself say when he and Garrett returned to the cart.

Garrett frowned. "Go with me? To England, ye mean?"

Finn nodded, heaving a deep sigh as Emma's image drifted into his mind. "Aye, to England." At first, it had only been Ian who'd been married and become a father, but now that Garrett, too, had lost his heart and married, Finn began to dread his own future with each passing day. For to him, it seemed that he would be forever doomed to yearn for a woman who did not want him. Would he never marry and have children of his own? Would he remain alone forever?

That thought sent a cold chill into his bones. As much as he wanted Emma, he knew he could not have her. But perhaps he could try and lose his heart to another. Somewhere, out in the world, there might be a woman who would could sweep him off his feet the same way Garrett's English lass had done for him.

Perhaps.

So far he had not found her during his visits to Clan MacKinnear. Was that because she was waiting for him in England? *Or right here at home?*

"Why?" Garrett asked, breaking into Finn's thoughts. "Ye've never spoken of going to England before. What brought on this thought?"

Finn sighed, "I...I...To tell ye the truth, I want what ye've already found," he told Garrett honestly. "I listen to the way ye speak about yer wife and I know that..."

Garrett nodded, grasping Finn's shoulder as he turned to look at him. "I understand what ye mean. Love's powerful." Shaking his head, he laughed. "It claimed me whole in a single night, and I tell ye honestly I didna see it coming."

Finn smiled, wishing his heart would simply have hope instead of reminding him of that one morning seven years ago when he had first noticed Emma.

"What about Emma?"

At Garrett's question, Finn flinched, wondering if Garrett, too, had developed the ability to read another's mind. Swallowing, he tried his best to pretend that his heart had not just danced wildly in his chest. "What about her?"

The corner of Garrett's mouth curled upward into a suspicious grin. "Dunno pretend that ye dunno care for the lass."

As his muscles clenched in shock, Finn tried to swallow the sudden lump in his throat. "What gave ye that idea? I barely know her."

Garrett laughed, "And *I* had never met my wife until the night of our wedding." He shook his head. "Nah, love doesna care about time, or right and wrong. It simply is...or not." For a split second, he glanced at Ian, and Finn wondered if he knew more than Ian had shared with him. "What about that kiss?"

Again, Finn flinched, annoyed with his inability to maintain a calm exterior. How did Cormag do it? Or did he truly never feel anything remotely resembling that which currently waged war in Finn's chest? "What kiss? Ye mean that quick peg seven years ago? That wasna a kiss! 'Twas nothing but a dare."

The moment the grin slid off Garrett's face, Finn wanted to kick himself for saying more than he had meant to.

"A dare?" Garrett asked, straightening as he had only just now leaned down to pick up another log. "Ye never told us that. How long have ye known?"

Finn shrugged, looking down at the snow-covered ground as the memory of that morning returned fresh and clear. "I've always known."

"Ye followed her that morning," Garrett mumbled, and Finn could feel his friend's eyes on him. "Did she tell ye that?"

Sighing, Finn met Garrett's gaze. "Nah, I overhead her speaking to her friends. She only did it to win the dare. 'Twas nothing more."

Garrett's gaze narrowed. "But 'twas for ye, was it not?" Finn scoffed, ready to deny his friend's suspicions with all the vehemence he could muster, but Garrett cut him off. "Why else would the lass affect ye so? Why else do ye keep glaring at her as though she's put a hex on ye? Why else do ye interfere with her life?"

Too thunderstruck to think straight, Finn gawked at his friend. "What?" was all he could manage.

"Last year," Garret supplied helpfully, his gaze narrowed as he watched Finn with a Cormag-like intensity, "ye told that fellow from Clan MacKinnear...what was his name?...Hamish, aye...ye told Hamish MacKinnear that the lass was promised. Why did ye do that when ye knew full well that it wasna true? Ye didna like the way he kept looking at her. Ye didna like it one bit. The glower ye always have about ye when she's near was never as dark as then. Admit it, ye care for her."

Overwhelmed at having all this pulled out into the open, Finn retreated a few paces when Ian drew near and reached for another log. Again, he glared at them before ploughing on through the snow to the next cottage while Cormag led the horse and cart a bit farther down the road.

"So, 'tis true then?" Garrett asked, a bit of a smug smile on his face as he stepped up to Finn. "Ye care for her? If that is so, why do ye wish to leave?"

"I never said I cared for her," Finn hissed under his breath as his hands curled into fists, trying desperately to hold on to his composure. "'Twas only a misunderstanding."

Garrett laughed, "Ye can say what ye wish, Finn, but no one glares at another like that without deep emotions. The lass must've truly gotten to ye. Why else would ye care what she does or who she marries?"

At the thought, every fibre in Finn's body tensed to the point of breaking, and for a long moment, he simply stood and stared at Garrett.

"Aye, I can see very well that she means nothing to ye," his friend mocked. "A bit of advice, dunno wait too long. One of these days, ye willna succeed in turning away a suitor, and then she'll be lost to ye. Why do ye think I married Claudia right then and there on the spot?" A large grin on his face, Garrett sighed. "She's a fierce woman, beautiful and strong and so...so verra alive. I knew another man might snatch her up in an instant, and so I claimed her as my own as fast as I could. No matter where she is, I will find her and remind her that she's mine...as I am hers." Garrett's eyes sobered. "Ye'd be wise to do the same...if indeed ye care for her." Then he stepped away and hurried after the cart, bending down to work again as a more-than-annoyed Ian glared at him.

"Ye'd do well to heed his advice."

Spinning around, Finn found Cormag standing behind him. "How long have ye been there?"

"Not long," Cormag replied, and yet, it seemed he knew all there was to know as he generally did. He inhaled a slow breath as his gaze once more travelled over Finn as though he was trying to make sense of something. "What does she mean to ye?"

Finn gritted his teeth, uncertain how he felt about the path his friends were urging him to take.

"I see," Cormag replied, seemingly satisfied with the answer he had glimpsed on Finn's face. Then he sighed, a hint of exhaustion coming to his grey eyes.

"What is it?" Finn asked, wishing he could read others as well as Cormag could, particularly Emma.

Cormag shrugged. "I canna help but wonder why people are so vehement in pretending that they dunno care, for it only seems to complicate matters."

Finn sighed. Leave it to Cormag to turn a heart's fears into a matter of the mind. Then he stopped, his gaze rising to meet his laird's. "People?" he mumbled, and his traitorous heart thudded loudly in his chest. "Ye said, *people*. Who did ye mean?"

Cormag's brows rose, and it was all the answer Finn needed. "Emma?" he whispered as his hands once more balled into fists, willing the hope in his heart to cease its conquest. "Did she...did she say anything to ye?"

"She didna have to," Cormag replied, "for the lass is as inept at pretending that she doesna care as ye are, Finn." For a short moment, a rather indulgent smile curved up Cormag's lips before he turned and walked away, returning to their task at hand.

Swallowing, Finn stared after him. Could it be true? Was there a chance that Emma harboured sentiments other than indifference and disregard for him? Whenever he saw her, she never turned to look at him, and whenever their eyes happened to meet, she always turned away with such haste as though the very sight of him offended her. Could there be another reason for her reaction as there was another reason for his own?

Certainly, he did not hate her. He hated that she did not care for him. That she had led him to believe that she did but had then crushed his hopes without a look back.

Or had he been wrong?

Intrigued and-heavens, yes!-hopeful, Finn knew that he needed to see her, perhaps even speak to her before he decided to leave. If he did not, he would spend the rest of his life wondering what could have been.

Chapter Three

OUT INTO THE SNOW

With only one day left until the annual yuletide feast at Seann Dachaigh Tower, the whole castle was abuzz: the hum of voices and hurrying feet echoing through the grand hall like bees in a hive. Furniture was moved to make room for rows upon rows of tables, all of which were in need of decorating to match the festive mood stirred by evergreens hung up in archways and around windows alike.

Emma and Maggie had spent the past two days decorating the hall, tying bows and stars fashioned out of straw into the evergreen branches to brighten up the castle. Still, Maggie was not satisfied, and a dark scowl came to her face when her eyes swept over the still-barren tables. "This won't do," she stated matter-of-factly, arms akimbo. "We need more branches."

Emma sighed, her fingers beginning to feel numb. "We dunno have any more." She gestured to the lush decorations around the hall. "I think 'tis enough, Maggie. Ye did a fine job. Ye should be proud."

Pressing her lips into a thin line, Maggie shook her head, disapproval clear in her blue eyes.

Due to her enthusiasm and utter commitment to the task, Maggie had taken over the planning of the yuletide feast five years ago...almost upon arriving in Scotland. At first, people had frowned at the young English lass, but soon everyone had been delighted with the way she flitted around the castle like a fairy, brightening everything she touched, her eyes aglow with joy.

Today, Maggie was as much a Scot as any one of them, and people often shook their heads at the thought that she had not grown up in the Highlands. *A minor detail*, Maggie generally called it. *A detail to be neglected.*

By now, people tended to agree.

"We need more branches," Maggie stated once more, and Emma knew better than to argue. "Niall, Blair," she called her children, who came rushing up with excitement, hoping to be entrusted with an important task. "Go find yer father. We need to go out into the woods to cut more branches." The children squealed with delight and immediately set off. "And tell him to bring Garrett and Finn," Maggie yelled after them.

Emma froze at the thought of Finn accompanying them. Generally, they tended to stay out of each other's way, only stumbling upon the other by accident.

"Dunno look so shocked," Maggie chided as she handed Emma her heavy winter cloak and then reached for her own as well as her children's. "I told ye ye needed to speak to him. Today is as good a day as any."

Staring at her friend, Emma swallowed. "Ye want me to talk to him?"

Maggie rolled her eyes. "Were ye not listening? What have we been talking about these past days?" Stepping closer, she held Emma's gaze. "Aye, I want ye to talk to him."

"But..." Emma could feel her skin crawl at the thought of Finn's glaring green eyes. "I thought...perhaps in the new year. I mean there's no rush, is there?"

"Aye, there is," Maggie objected as she rushed down the corridor leading out into the courtyard.

Pulling her cloak around herself, Emma hastened after her. "There is? Why? What do ye mean?"

As they stepped out into the cold, they saw Maggie's children running toward them, their father in their tow...as well as Garrett, Finn...and Vaughn. Emma groaned inwardly.

"What were ye thinking rushing outside without bundling up first?" Maggie chided her children, their noses bright red from the cold. Quickly, she wrapped Blair in a warm winter cloak and handed Niall his lined coat. "Ye'll be sorry when we're all at the feast and ye'll be in bed with a cold."

Shock widened the children's eyes; however, only for a moment. Soon, they were running through the snow once more, giggling and laughing.

"What did ye mean?" Emma whispered in Maggie's ear as she watched the men approach, wondering at the way Finn glared not at her, but at Vaughn instead. Dimly, she wondered what the young man had done to draw Finn's wrath. She doubted he had stolen a kiss as well. In fact, his eyes were on her, and a large smile drew up the corners of his mouth.

Emma sighed, disappointment filling her heart.

While Finn did little else but glare in her direction if, indeed, he paid her any attention, Vaughn always smiled at her, his eyes lighting up with joy. In fact, he had been smiling at her for a while now, and Emma was beginning to think that soon he might muster the courage to ask for her hand. Still, Emma could not deny that Vaughn's warm brown eyes never managed to set her blood on fire the way Finn's dark green blaze did.

Oh, why could she not have lost her heart to Vaughn instead?

"Ian told me," Maggie whispered as they descended the front steps, "that Finn asked to accompany Garret to England."

Emma froze as though the snow around her feet had suddenly frozen into a block of ice, stopping her progress.

Turning back, Maggie looked at her, a teasing smile coming to her lips. "Aye, I can see that he means nothing to ye."

Swallowing, Emma reached for Maggie's arm and pulled her to her side. "Why?" was all she could ask as her heart beat painfully in her chest at the thought of Finn disappearing from her life.

Maggie's face sobered, and her blue eyes shone with compassion. "To find himself a bride."

Pain shot through Emma's middle, and her knees felt as though they would give out any moment. Her hands grasped Maggie's, and she had to lean heavily on her dainty friend lest she drop to the ground.

"Are ye all right?" came Vaughn's concerned voice as he rushed to their side, his warm brown eyes searching her face. "Ye look pale. Is anything wrong?"

Swallowing the lump in her throat, Emma assured him that she was fine when Finn's scowling face appeared beside Vaughn's. His eyes were hard as they met hers, and Emma did not dare look at him a moment longer.

"The bairns said ye needed more branches," Ian cut in, his gaze wandering over the various expressions on their faces before his own joined Finn's, taking on a displeased scowl. "Are ye sure ye dunno have enough?"

Maggie rolled her eyes at her husband. "D'ye think I would drag all of ye out here for nothing. Aye, I need more branches. So, let's be off."

Grumbling something under his breath, Ian went off to hitch a horse to the small cart with runners that they used whenever the snow got too deep. While Finn went after him, Garrett chased Niall and Blair around the yard.

"Perhaps ye should stay here," Vaughn suggested, his eyes still holding concern as he looked at Emma. "Ye still look pale. Perhaps ye need rest."

Maggie smiled at him, gently patting Emma's hand. "She'll be fine. There's no need to worry." She glanced at her children flinging snowballs at a downed Garrett. "Would ye mind helping him out? He looks to be in need of aid."

Turning to look over his shoulder, Vaughn laughed and then hurried off to lend a hand.

"He's right," Maggie said after returning her gaze to Emma. "Ye look pale."

Gritting her teeth, Emma felt tears brimming in the corners of her eyes, and it took all her willpower to keep them from rolling down her chilled cheeks. "I'm fine," she whispered as though she could will those words to be true.

"Aye, I can see that," Maggie replied, disbelief clear in her voice.

"Come, let's get to work." Then she looped her arm through Emma's and together with the children followed after Ian as he guided the horse and cart out through the front gate and toward the woods.

Emma's heart and mind felt numb as she trudged onward through the snow, the children's voices echoing around her as they laughed and cheered, enjoying the winter wonderland around them. Vaughn stayed by her side, his calm voice soothing even though Emma could not concentrate on the words he spoke.

On they walked until they left the path and cut deeper into the woods where the trees were still untouched. Ian called them to a halt and ordered them to spread out. Since they would not cut down another tree and then use its branches for decorating the hall, the plan was to cut individual branches off trees here and there.

"Talk to him," Maggie whispered into Emma's ear before she nodded to the west where Finn was disappearing between the trees. "Now." Maggie's steely blue eyes did not allow for an argument before she turned to Vaughn, who still hovered nearby, and drew his attention away, setting him to work.

An insistent shove sent Emma on her way, and she reluctantly stumbled through the snow, her feet as cold as ice. The last time she had sought Finn out on an equally cold day, all had ended in a disaster. That day, she had angered him. And yet, here she was, going after a man who clearly could not care less about her. Why on earth did Maggie insist she subject herself to this torture? Was it not clear that Finn had set his sights elsewhere?

Again, the day of her father's burial surfaced in her mind, and instantly, her traitorous heart had hope.

Cursing under her breath, Emma stumbled onward, trying her best to convince herself that Finn's kindness that day had indeed been nothing else but that, kindness.

Her eyes fell on branch after branch as she followed in Finn's wake. A distant part of her mind urged her to pick them up, reminding her of why they had come out here in the first place. Still, Emma could not bring herself to heed those thoughts as she was too busy trying to hold utter panic at bay. What on earth was she doing following him? What was there to say? What should she-?

"Oh!"

It was nothing more than a breathy sound that escaped her lips as her eyes fell on Finn. He stood beside a large fir tree, in the process of cutting off one of the lower-hanging branches. His hands were steady, and the rhythmic sounds of the saw ought to have alerted her to his presence even before she had stumbled upon him. Her mind, however, had been too distracted.

Finn, too, seemed to have been elsewhere with his thoughts for the moment her breathy "oh" filled the air, he flinched as though a shot had been fired near his head. His right hand slipped, and the saw's teeth scraped over the back of his other hand, drawing blood.

A curse flew from his lips as he spun around, holding his injured hand to his chest. Then his eyes met hers, and he all but stumbled backwards until his back collided with the tree. His chest rose and fell with rapid breaths, and yet, his gaze remained hard.

More than anything, Emma wanted to turn around and run, but the sight of a drop of his blood running down his hand and dripping into the snow held her in place. "I'm sorry," she whispered, her suddenly warm feet carrying her closer. "I didna mean to startle ye."

Finn's teeth gritted together as he stared at her, seemingly at a loss for words.

Still, Emma stepped closer, wondering where the sudden courage had come from to approach him in such a direct fashion. Perhaps it was not courage, she thought as her gaze once more dropped to his injured hand. Perhaps it was simply that his pain was hers, and she could not bear it.

"Let me help ye." Drawing a handkerchief from her pocket, Emma approached him, her eyes on his to gauge if her doing so would displease him. Although his eyes remained hard, he did not object nor draw away.

When she came to stand in front of him, Emma had to lift her chin to look up into his eyes. It had been seven years since they had last stood this close together, and his warm breath as it fell onto her skin sent tantalising shivers down her back.

A sudden desire rushed through Emma's body, and for a moment, she feared she would lose all control and kiss him again.

Biting her lip, she forced her eyes down to his injured hand. "It's not deep," she mumbled as she gently wrapped her handkerchief around his hand, tying a small knot to keep it in place. "I think ye'll live," she whispered as her eyes found his once more, a hint of humour in her voice that surprised her as much as him.

For a split second, his lips seemed to quiver as though wishing to curl up into a smile, and Emma's heart almost leapt out of her chest.

"What are ye doing here?" Finn suddenly asked, his sharp voice cutting through the soft bond Emma had felt in her heart. "Should ye not be by Vaughn's side?"

As though slapped, Emma took a step back. "Vaughn? No, I..." She glanced at the branches in the snow. "I came to help ye collect these."

Stepping away from her, Finn picked up the two branches by his feet. "There's no need. I can manage."

Coldness reclaimed Emma's body, and her foolish heart sank. "I heard ye plan to go to England with Garrett." *Wherever had that come from?*

Finn blinked, his gaze returning to hers as his brows drew down. "Where did ye hear that?"

"Is it not true?" Emma pressed, cursing her tongue for it would only get her in trouble. And yet, she had to know if what Maggie had said would indeed come to pass.

Crossing his arms, Finn cocked an eyebrow, clearly unwilling to answer her unless she answered him first.

"Maggie told me," Emma finally said, feeling her heart calm with the familiar back and forth of conversation. "I believe she heard it from Ian. Why? Was it to be a secret?"

Inhaling a deep breath, Finn shrugged. "Nah, I'm merely surprised ye know as I only mentioned it the other day." He sighed, and for a reason Emma could not understand, his face suddenly darkened. "News travels fast, 'twould seem."

Emma nodded, knowing very well that secrets rarely lasted long in their clan. "Why do ye wish to go to England?" Her hands shook, and so she curled them around one another under her cloak.

Finn scoffed, "What is it to ye?"

Gritting her teeth, Emma glared at him, annoyed with the way he always seemed to antagonise her. "Why do ye get angry? I merely asked a question. Is that so bad?"

The muscles in Finn's jaw seemed to pulse as he stared back at her. Then all of a sudden, his features softened, and the air rushed from his lungs as though he had been holding it. "Listen, I-"

"Emma?"

At the sound of Vaughn's voice nearby, Emma could have groaned. Even if only for a moment, she wanted nothing more but to speak to Finn and have him speak to her, not as though they were enemies but with kindness. She would give anything to have him once more look at her the way he had the day of her father's burial. The softness and compassion in his eyes had been breath-taking, and Emma had longed for it for years.

Now, that hope seemed to be dashed as his green gaze hardened, his arms returning to cross over his chest as though to keep her away at all cost. "'Tis none of yer concern why I do anything, ye hear," he growled, his voice as hard as ever before he stalked off, leaving nothing but prints in the snow.

Chapter Four

ALL IS FAIR IN LOVE AND WAR

S torming away, Finn knew that he was acting like a headstrong bairn, unwilling to discuss what bothered him. And yet, if he had stayed a moment longer, he would have acted like a boorish man, yanking her into his arms, claiming her as his and kissing her the way he had wanted to for seven long years.

Ever since that cold winter's morning when she had surprised him, stunned him witless...and stolen not only a kiss, but his heart as well.

Emma, however, had not wanted him that morning. All she had wanted was to win a game, a dare. She had not wanted him then, and she did not now. Not once since that day had she done anything that would have suggested her feelings on the matter had changed.

Cursing under his breath, Finn curled his good hand around the handkerchief she had put on his scraped knuckles. The pain was minimal, and the cuts would have needed no bandaging. Still, he could not deny that the concern he had seen in her eyes had once again rendered him speechless. It had touched him, and he had wanted to believe that she cared, that his pain had touched her as well.

Her eyes had been so kind and tender as she had looked up at him, her warm hand brushing over his skin as she had seen to his wound. His body had responded instantly, and his heart had hammered in his chest wildly, urging him to finally address her. Would it truly be worse to have her reject him? To know with certainty that she did not care? Or was the sliver of hope he clung to something he needed in order to survive?

Ready to put his heart on the line, Finn had let down his defences, knowing that he could not live with uncertainty for the rest of his life...when Vaughn's voice had shattered all his hopes.

Anger had curled around his heart in an instant, and his defences had come back up. More than once he had seen Vaughn smile at Emma, and every now and then, she had even smiled back at him.

Upon seeing it, Finn had almost doubled over in pain, and it had been in that moment that he had realised he had indeed lost his heart to her.

Absolutely and irrevocably.

"I need to leave," Finn grumbled as he stomped through the snow with no regard for where he was headed. Not once had she smiled at him. "I need to go."

"Finn? Is that ye?"

Stopping in his tracks, Finn turned toward Ian's voice before his friend stepped out from behind a thicket, his gaze narrowing as he took in the scowl on Finn's face. "What's wrong?" His gaze darted to Finn's wrapped hand. "Are ye hurt? I would've thought ye knew how to handle a saw."

Finn scoffed, remembering that he had left it lying in the snow. "'Tis nothing."

"'Tis not nothing." Rolling his eyes, Ian heaved a deep sigh. "'Tis Emma, is it not?"

Finn opened his mouth to object, but Ian waved him off. "D'ye know that Vaughn intends to ask for her hand?"

Shock barrelled into Finn like a charging boar. Although he had suspected-anyone would have-having it confirmed was a thousand times more agonising. "He d-?" He swallowed the lump in his throat as his injured hand suddenly ached painfully. "Why would I care?" The words fell from his lips to lie dead at his feet.

Ian heaved another deep sigh; annoyance and a hint of anger clear on his face. "It doesna matter why ye care, Finn. All that matters is that ye do. Ye care about her whether ye like it or not." A growl rose from Ian's throat, and his jaw clenched. "Ye make me so angry."

"Why?" Finn asked, rather surprised by his friend's emotional involvement in this matter. "What is it to ye?"

"Ye're not being fair!" Ian snapped, his eyes narrowed as he approached. "What ye both are doing is not fair! Ye're being selfish and...and fools on top of it."

Never had Finn seen his friend lose his temper quite like this. Although Ian was known to have strong opinions and tended to argue with vehemence, the way he spoke to Finn now was different. It was as though the outcome of this personally affected him.

"What do ye mean?" Finn asked, wondering about the bitterness that had grown in his friend over the last few years. "She and I are nothing to each other. We-"

Ian laughed, but it was a mirthless laugh. "Truly?" He shook his head, utter disbelief in his eyes. "Everybody knows how ye two feel about one another. Why is it that *ye* canna see it?" He took a step forward, his gaze burning with challenge. "Tell me, would ye truly not care if Emma married Vaughn? Would ye dance at their wedding as ye danced at mine?"

Ian's question felt like a renewed blow to his mid-section, and Finn merely stood and stared at his friend while another part of him could not help but return to what Ian had said before. *Everybody knows how ye two feel about one another. Why is it that ye canna see it?*

Was there truth in Ian's words? Or was he merely angry and-? But why would he say something like that without truly believing it to be true? What reason could he have? After all, Ian was one of his oldest friends. They had always gone through thick and thin together. Finn had no reason to doubt his word.

"Nah," Ian said, shaking his head rather absentmindedly, as his fingers tensed around the axe in his hand. "She shouldna marry him. She shouldna!"

Strangely relieved to have another agree, Finn nodded. "Aye, they dunno suit. He's too-"

"They shouldna marry," Ian hissed, advancing on Finn with a blazing fire in his eyes, "because she doesna love him! That's why! If she marries him, she'll doom Vaughn to a loveless marriage, tied to someone whose heart he canna win. Does that seem fair to ye?"

Stunned, Finn looked at his friend, and for the first time, Ian's anger and bitterness seemed to make sense. "Does Maggie-?"

"It doesna matter!" Ian snapped, his chest rising and falling with each agitated breath. His hand was still clenched around the axe he held, and his jaw was tense to the point of breaking. Still, it seemed he was fighting to regain control and calm the emotions that had all of a sudden run wild. "Ye still have a chance," he finally said, his body strung tight, but his voice quiet, almost breathless. "Ye still have a chance to be happy. Dunno waste it, and dunno doom others because ye're afraid."

Finn swallowed, overcome with the sorrow he saw in Ian's eyes. "Thank ye, my friend, for speaking so plainly. I canna say anyone ever has."

Ian nodded. "Then do us both a favour and heed my advice. Dunno thank me and then carry on as though ye havena heard a word I said."

"Did ye truly mean what ye said?" Finn asked, remembering the way Emma sometimes smiled at Vaughn, the way he gazed at her like a love-struck fool. Finn could not for the life of him remember her ever smiling at him. Did that not mean that her heart belonged to Vaughn? "How can I be certain she cares?"

Ian's lips pressed into a thin line as he once more rolled his eyes at Finn. Then he took a step closer, his blue eyes dark and thunderous as they held Finn's. "Go and ask her!" he snapped, his voice cutting through the still winter air like a whip. Then he spun on his heel and walked away, his angry footsteps dulled by the soft snow covering the ground.

Chapter Five

SILENT SORROW

"**S**orry," Maggie mumbled as she hastened toward Emma, her arms filled with cut branches. "I turned my head once, and he slipped through my fingers." As she lowered her treasures into the cart, her gaze travelled to Vaughn, who had come walking back with Emma a few minutes ago and was now attempting to chop another branch off a fir tree.

"'Tis all right," Emma mumbled, unable to hide her anger and disappointment. "Finn was a horrid person. No matter what I do, he always snaps at me as though my presence alone offends him." She shook her head, willing anger to supersede disappointment. "If he canna even be civil, then there's no point in talking to him." She scoffed, her hands coming up to rest on her sides as righteous indignation spread through her heart, pushing aside the pain that tended to linger. "I canna stand him one bit, and I feel awfully sorry for the poor English lass he'll choose for his bride."

Finished with her tirade, Emma turned to Maggie and found her friend all but glaring at her, her bright blue eyes dark and filled with utter annoyance. "Ye're a fool," Maggie hissed, grabbing Emma's arm and pulling her aside. Glancing around them, she dropped her voice to a whisper. "Why do ye so stubbornly ignore how ye feel? Why can ye not see that Finn cares for ye? Are ye truly blind? Or do ye enjoy having two men vie for yer hand?"

Shocked, Emma blinked. "What do ye mean?" Never had she seen Maggie quite this agitated, this angry, this...hurt. "Two men? 'Tis only Vaughn who-"

Gritting her teeth, sweet, cheerful Maggie seemed to be fighting for control. "D'ye truly think 'tis a coincidence that the moment Vaughn started smiling at ye, Finn couldna seem to stand the man any longer? He's jealous," she hissed, her blue eyes holding Emma's as though wanting to make certain that her friend understood.

Emma swallowed, ignoring the little dance her heart was currently performing in her chest. "Jealous? Nah, ye canna mean that. He hates me. He only ever glares at me. He has ever since that morning when-"

"Oh, I wish I had known ye back then," Maggie interrupted, hands gesturing wildly as she began to pace. "I wish I'd come to Seann Dachaigh Tower a year earlier. I wish I'd been here for I would've pushed ye to seek him out again the next day and steal another kiss."

"What?"

Maggie stopped, her eyes hard, before she walked over to Emma with sure steps until their noses almost touched. "I'll never believe he's been angry with ye for all these years because ye kissed him. That's nonsense. Even if he hadn't liked it, he wouldna have acted like that. He would've laughed it off and gone on his merry way." Maggie's breath came in rapid gasps, and for a moment, she closed her eyes and then inhaled a deep breath. "Perhaps I should've spoken to ye sooner, pushed ye to see what is right in front of yer eyes." Looking at Emma, Maggie sighed, her eyes now brimming with tears. "I didna because I didna think 'twas my place to meddle in other people's affairs." Her lips pressed into a tight line, and for a moment, Emma thought she saw a memory cross over Maggie's face. "Others often think they know what's right, but they dunno. They push and they prod until they get what they want, and then...ye choose the wrong path and all is lost."

Misery now stood on Maggie's face, and Emma walked over pulling her friend into her arms. At first, the slender young woman resisted, but then her head sank down onto Emma's shoulder and she inhaled a shuddering breath. "I'm sorry for yer pain," Emma whispered into Maggie's auburn hair, wondering what had happened in her friend's past. Never had Maggie spoken of anything that would explain the pain and loss she had seen in her blue eyes just now.

All people ever talked about was how Maggie had come to Scotland to visit her mother's clan and then had stayed because she had fallen in love with Ian MacDrummond and married him.

That was the story Emma knew, but apparently there was more to it than she ever would have thought.

Pulling back, Maggie ran her hands over her eyes and wiped away her tears. "Ye think too much, Emma," she said, the ghost of a smile tugging on the corners of her lips. "Nothing good ever comes of it when people think too much. The heart wants what it wants, and no amount of reasonable thinking or good intentions can change that." Grasping Emma's hands, Maggie looked at her, her eyes intense, almost pleading. "Ye're lucky, Emma. Ye still have a chance to marry the man ye love, and if that man is Vaughn, then I willna say another word." Her hands squeezed Emma's. "But if it's not, then please, please, go and speak to Finn. Tell him how ye feel, or ye will regret it for the rest of yer life." She swallowed. "I promise ye that."

Holding her friend's gaze, Emma felt her limbs begin to tremble. With what, she could not say. Maggie's sorrow touched her, frightened her, and yet, the thought of laying open her heart and have Finn stomp on it scared her nearly witless. "Is there anything I can do?" she whispered, searching Maggie's face. "D'ye wish to talk about-?"

"No," Maggie said vehemently. "I've made my choice. What's done is done. But ye're still at the beginning of yer story. Make certain ye choose the right man or it will turn into a tragedy, and I dunno want that for ye." After squeezing Emma's hands one last time, Maggie returned to the cart, accepting a bunch of branches from Niall and Blair, who loved dragging them through the snow, giggling as they went.

Watching them, Emma was struck by the peacefulness of the sight before her, and yet, the look on Maggie's face whispered of falsehood.

Certainly, she loved her children, but quite obviously, she had not married the man she loved.

Emma sighed, wondering if she possessed the strength to do what Maggie had not.

Chapter Six

DEFINITIONS OF A KISS

As the sky slowly grew darker, they all gathered around the cart, making certain no one was left behind. Then they began the long walk back to Seann Dachaigh Tower. Once again, Finn's insides twisted into a tight knot when he saw Vaughn approach Emma. The man fell in step beside her, speaking animatedly while Emma seemed distracted, her gaze distant.

Again, Finn contemplated Ian's words as well as the vehemence with which his friend had spoken. Still, uncertainty remained, and Finn knew that there was only one way to rid himself of it. He needed to speak to Emma.

Tonight.

All of a sudden, after seven long years, Finn could not wait any longer. He needed to know so that he could make his choice in the best way possible.

Once they reached the courtyard, their little group broke apart. While Ian positioned the cart near the back entrance to the hall and then returned the horse to the stables, Maggie and Emma took the children inside to warm up. Vaughn took his leave, mumbling something about returning later, and walked down to the village where his family lived in one of the larger cottages.

"Ye'll speak to her, won't ye?" Garrett observed, a bit of a smirk on his face as he watched Finn.

Turning toward his friend, Finn sighed. "What gave me away?"

Garrett chuckled, "I dunno know. I guess 'tis the look in yer eyes. Determined, and yet...terrified."

Finn laughed, "Ye sound as though ye know the feeling well?"

"Aye," Garrett replied with a deep sigh. "Love will do that to ye. But it'll also make ye feel alive in a way ye've never felt before." Then he patted Finn on the back, wished him good luck and walked off.

Heading into the hall, Finn kept to the shadows, watching as Maggie and Emma as well as a few other volunteers returned to their task of decorating the rows upon rows of tables set out for tomorrow's feast. Evergreen branches were tied together and placed in the middle, then adorned with red ribbons and straw figurines. In between, they placed large candles. At first, Niall and Blair tried to help, but soon they lay passed out in a corner of the hall near the large fireplace, sound asleep.

Finn waited; however, not patiently as the mere sight of Emma so near, and yet, so far away was torture.

Before, he had always done his utmost not to be near her, to avoid her wherever possible, and whenever they had stumbled upon one another after all, he had always retreated as fast as he could have without truly giving offence. Never had he simply stood and looked at her, watched the way her brows furrowed when she was concentrating, the way her teeth sunk into her lower lip when she was getting agitated, or the way her eyes shone when she looked down at Niall and Blair, gently draping her cloak over the sleeping children.

She was magnificent, and Finn knew very well why he had never allowed himself to see her thus.

He was so lost in his thoughts that he almost failed to notice when Emma slipped from the hall, taking the corridor toward the back entrance. Presumably, Maggie had sent her to fetch more branches. Could there possibly be any left? Who on earth needed all these decorations? They would wither and die soon anyhow.

Pushing himself off the wall he had been leaning against, Finn hurried after her, careful not to draw Maggie's attention. Quick strides carried him onward, and he came upon Emma as she was about to step outside. "Emma," he called before all courage could desert him.

At the sound of his voice, she turned to look at him, utter surprise in her gaze. "Finn, what are ye doing here? I thought ye'd left with Garrett."

The thought that she paid attention to his whereabouts pleased him, and he could not prevent a smile from showing on his face.

Seeing it, her gaze narrowed in confusion, and yet, the way her breath rushed from her lungs and the corners of her mouth drew upward ever so slightly spoke of joy. Did she truly care about him? Was it possible that Ian was right? That he had been ever so blind?

Her eyes held his, and belatedly, Finn realised that he ought to say something. "I...I wanted to speak to ye," he began, cursing the way his voice shook. "I need to speak to ye."

"Aye?" Her eyes remained on his, waiting, expecting...hopeful somehow, and yet, guarded.

Finn knew only too well how that felt. Where on earth was he to begin? He could not very well ask her straight out if she cared for him, could he? Would she not laugh at him?

Clearing his throat, he groped for words. "I wanted to...I've heard... that is, I've heard that Vaughn intends to ask for yer hand." The moment the words had left his lips, Finn could have kicked himself. Poorer words had never been chosen, that much was certain.

As expected, the glow in her eyes dimmed, and her arms rose to cross in front of her chest...as though to put a barrier between them, to keep him away. "I fail to see how 'tis any of yer business." Her voice was harsh as she spoke, and yet, he thought to detect a hint of pain as well.

"I'm sorry I blurted it out like that," Finn apologised as best as he could while his nerves lay bare, "but I need to know if ye intend to marry him."

Exhaling a quick breath, she frowned. "Why? Why do ye *need* to know? What is it to ye?"

"I just..." Gritting his teeth, Finn took a step closer, his gaze unable to veer from hers. "I simply need to know."

Scoffing, she shook her head. "Why? If I didna know any better, I'd think ye're jealous."

Her words were like a stab to his heart, and Finn momentarily dropped his gaze. When his eyes found hers once more, the look on her face was one of sheer incredulity. Oh, dear god, she knew! Would she laugh at him now?

"It c-canna be," she stammered, her warm brown eyes fixed on his. "Ye hate me. Ye always glare at me. We're nothing to each other. We've barely spoken a word to each other since-" Her voice broke off, and she dropped her gaze as heat shot up her face, colouring her cheeks a crimson red.

Finn rejoiced, his heart hammering in his chest as he stepped closer, undeniably drawn to the woman with the dark brown eyes who had been haunting his dreams for years. "Since that morning," he whispered, "although ye did not say much."

Emma swallowed, lifting her chin a fraction, a hint of righteous indignation coming to her voice. "Neither did ye. Ye only stood and stared."

"Aye." Finn nodded, a small smile claiming his features. "Aye, I did. I admit ye threw me off balance."

The red in her cheeks darkened. "I'm sorry. I...I shouldna have kissed ye. I..."

"'Twas not a true kiss," Finn said, watching her closely.

Her gaze narrowed, and a frown drew down her brows. "What do ye mean? Of course, 'twas a kiss. What else could it have been?"

Holding her gaze, he leaned closer. "A dare."

Shock widened her eyes and dropped her jaw. "Ye kn-know?" she stammered. "How?"

Emma's heart pounded in her ears like a stampede as she stared up at Finn, mortified by his rightful accusation. Ever since Maggie had spoken to her so honestly, Emma had heard her friend's words echoing in her mind. *I'll never believe he's been angry with ye for all these years because*

ye kissed him. That's nonsense. Even if he hadn't liked it, he wouldna have acted like that. He would've laughed it off and gone on his merry way.

But now she knew why he had been angry, why he had glared at her all these years. And yet, it seemed an awfully long time to hold a grudge. Could it be that he cared for her? That he had been offended to think that *she* had not cared? That it had only been a dare to her? A game?

Could the answer truly be that simple?

"I followed ye," he answered her question, his eyes searching as though he, too, was looking for answers. "I followed ye, and I heard ye speaking to yer friends."

"Oh." If possible, Emma's cheeks burnt even hotter. "I'm sorry I..." Then a thought struck, and her eyes narrowed with renewed purpose. "Why did ye follow me?" she demanded, taking a step toward him, her eyes searching his. "Why?"

He swallowed, and she could sense that he wanted nothing more but to drop his gaze. But he did not. Instead, he squared his shoulders and accepted her challenge, offering one of his own. "Why did ye kiss me if indeed 'twas a kiss?"

Knowing his question to be a distraction, Emma still could not keep herself from taking the bait. "Of course, 'twas. Our lips touched, did they not?"

All of a sudden, the memory of their kiss loomed between them. Emma could see it in the green blaze that lit up his eyes, and her heart jumped into her throat when Finn's lips curled up into a wicked smile and his gaze dropped to her mouth for the barest of moments. "Have ye been kissed since that morning?"

Emma swallowed before a triumphant smile lit up her face. "Aha! So, ye admit that 'twas a kiss!"

Finn chuckled, and Emma could not remember ever having seen him like this. Not since that morning. Not in the past seven years. At least not around her.

Also, she could not help but wonder at what point they had come to stand almost nose to nose with little between them except thin air. "Answer me," Finn teased, his green eyes glowing with delight. "Has anyone kissed ye since?" His gaze darkened. "Has Vaughn?"

Squaring her shoulders, Emma looked him directly in the eyes. "Ye didn't answer me, either. Why did ye follow-?"

"Emma!" he all but growled, shooting toward her so that she had to take an involuntary step backwards to avoid collision. His hands reached for her, and before she knew what was happening, she was wrapped in his arms, his mouth a hair's breadth away from hers. "Has he kissed ye?"

Although her knees were shaking, Emma had to admit she liked the fierceness in him. "Why d'ye think ye can-?"

"Emma!"

"No!" she blurted out. "There. Happy now?"

An amused smile came to his face, and a chuckle rumbled deep in his throat. "Aye," Finn whispered as his eyes held hers. "Aye, I'm happy."

Locked in his embrace, Emma felt her breath come faster as his green gaze remained on hers, his arms keeping her steady, keeping her from sinking to the ground as her knees turned to water.

"Would ye object," Finn began, a slight quiver in the way he drew in another breath, "if I were to kiss ye right here, right now?"

The air flew from Emma's lungs as she tried to make sense of his words. Her head spun, and her heart raced, overwhelmed by the past few minutes she had so unexpectedly shared with Finn. They seemed like something out of a dream, and her mind had trouble believing that she was indeed awake. Still, he felt so real.

Never had she seen the green in his gaze more vibrant than in that moment as he held her gaze, waiting for her answer.

Trying to ignore the lump in her throat, Emma willed her chin to remain up. "Why would ye?" she demanded, willing a touch of haughtiness into her tone even though her body urged her to simply accept his offering.

After all, it had been seven years! Seven years full of dreams and hopes...and disappointment.

Finn chuckled, wickedness gleaming in his eyes. "So ye know what a true kiss feels like."

Emma's gaze narrowed. "I do know," she insisted, annoyed with the condescension that rang in his voice.

"No, ye dunno."

Her back straightened, and she pulled away, glaring up at him. "Aye, I d-"

"'Twas a dare," Finn insisted as he lowered his face to hers, his arms pulling her back against him. "'Twas only a dare."

Emma swallowed. Of course, she could tell him the truth. Tell him how much she had always cared for him. Tell him that the dare had only been a welcome excuse to kiss him. Tell him that she had feared for her heart if he were to reject her. Tell him it had been a mere way to save face. Tell him all that and more.

Still, despite the past few moments which had been nothing short of heaven on earth, Emma could not. Her heart still feared that she had strayed into a dream, that she was in this very moment misunderstanding his intentions, that now he might be the one acting upon a dare. "How condescending of ye," she hissed, steeling her voice, "to think ye know bet-"

The rest of her words were lost when his lips claimed hers, silencing her objections, her excuses, her protest.

Time stopped as they stood by the back door, his arms around her and his lips a gentle pressure on hers. Emma could hear her heart thundering in her ears and felt Finn's beat against the palm of her hand as it rested on his chest. Stillness fell over them as it had seven years ago, freezing them in place, their thoughts and emotions overwhelmed by something they had not seen coming.

Emma sighed, counting the seconds his lips remained on hers, expecting him to pull back any moment now as she had seven years ago.

But, he did not.

Instead, his lips grew more daring, moving over hers with bold curiosity. Again, she sighed, and he walked her back against the wall, his hands brushing over her arms, her back, her shoulders before reaching for her face. She felt the tips of his fingers tracing the line of her jaw and down the column of her neck. Tingles surged across her skin, and her blood felt as though it had been set on fire.

When Finn finally did pull back, his breath came fast, and his gaze remained locked on hers. "D'ye concede?" he asked, a teasing grin curling up his lips as he held her in his arms.

Rolling her eyes, Emma chuckled. "Aye, I concede. Ye were right. Now, kiss me again." Her fingers curled into the front of his shirt as she pulled him back toward her, enjoying the laughter that spilled from his mouth.

"As my lady desires," he whispered against her lips, a teasing tone in his voice. Always had he seemed so serious, rather glum and melancholy-at least whenever they'd crossed paths in the past seven years-that Emma knew not what to make of this passionate man who held her in his arms.

But she was more than willing to find out.

"Emma?"

At the sound of Maggie's voice echoing down the corridor toward them, Emma and Finn stumbled apart as though burnt. For a long second, they stared at one another as the magic of the previous moment faded away and reality caught up with them. Neither one of them knew what to say, and before Emma's mind could form a clear thought, Finn stepped away toward the door.

"Emma? Where are ye?"

Finn's eyes were full of things unsaid, and although Emma wished he would stay, she knew that the moment they had shared with each other had not settled things. In fact, Emma felt as unbalanced as never before, and she could see the same confusion on Finn's face as he stepped through the door and into the cold.

Chapter Seven
SUBTLE SIGNS OF LOVE

Carrying yet another armload of freshly-cut evergreen branches, Emma was lost in thought as she walked back to the great hall with Maggie by her side. Her lips still tingled from Finn's kiss, and rather begrudgingly, she had to admit that it had felt utterly overwhelming, a far cry from the soft peck she had given Finn all those years ago.

Was that why he had thought her unfeeling? Because she had lacked the ability to kiss him with such finesse? Was that why he had doubted her? Had his kiss today changed anything between them? Did he have any intentions towards her? After all, he had been relieved to hear that Vaughn had never kissed her. And had he not said he needed to know if she intended to marry Vaughn?

Had he not looked utterly jealous?

Emma's heart skipped a beat as hope once more surged forward, tickling the corners of her mouth and willing a smile onto her face that felt all the more overwhelming as it had been absent these past few years.

"Something happened," Maggie observed, her eyes narrowed as she watched Emma. "Tell me."

Swallowing, Emma turned to look at her friend. "I dunno know what ye mean," she mumbled, uncertain how to put into words the many contradicting emotions that lived in her heart.

Maggie chuckled, "'Tis Finn, isn't it?" Her eyes narrowed even further as though she could truly read Emma's thoughts. "What happened? Did he...did he kiss ye?" She glanced over her shoulder, back down the way they had come. "Just now? Was that why ye were gone for so long?"

Gritting her teeth, Emma felt heat rise to her cheeks, and mortified, she closed her eyes.

Maggie laughed, putting a gentle hand on Emma's shoulder. "Don't be embarrassed. I'm so happy for ye." Eagerness stood on her face. "How did it happen? Tell me everything."

Setting down the branches, Emma shook her head, her thoughts still running rampant as though she had no control over them. "How did ye know?" she asked in return, trying to distract Maggie from asking more questions Emma did not know how to answer.

A deep sigh full of longing and...remembrance left Maggie's lips. "Love is impossible to hide," she whispered, "at least from those not affected by it." Gently, she squeezed Emma's hand. "I can see it in ye and Finn because my heart isna burdened by doubt and fear. Ye may try to hide how ye feel, but those attempts make the truth even more obvious."

Emma nodded, wondering how she could ever have thought that Finn did not care for her. Now, it seemed only too obvious that there was something between them, that there had always been something between them. Why else would he have been so angry with her for so long? Still, a small part of Emma did not dare believe her own conclusions to be true. Maggie was right. Fear could be utterly blinding. "He did kiss me," she whispered, a shy smile on her face as she confided in her friend. "He seemed so different. I've never seen him like that. I dunno know what to believe. I mean, I know what I wish to be true, but..."

Again, Maggie squeezed her hand in reassurance. "Believe it for 'tis true. I promise ye." Nodding her head in affirmation, Maggie glanced around the hall until her eyes fell on Garrett as he stood by the far wall, speaking to Cormag. "Dunno tell me," Maggie said, a grin coming to her face, "that ye dunno know who Garrett is speaking about."

Emma smiled. "His wife."

"Aye," Maggie agreed. "'Tis in the way his eyes sparkle, the way his face lights up at the mere mention of her, the way his voice grows heavy with emotion when he speaks of her. 'Tis easy to see, is it not?"

Sighing, Emma nodded, her eyes on Garrett as he spoke to Cormag, his green eyes alight with longing-the same longing she had seen in Finn's eyes only moments ago? Oh, if only she could be certain.

"Ye can see it in Cormag as well," Maggie threw in, her eyes narrowing as she watched their laird. "His signs are more subtle, but they're there."

"Cormag?" Emma frowned as her gaze drifted to the stoic leader of their clan. Although his eyes always seemed wide open, watchful, aware of everything that went on around him, he never seemed affected by any of it. Never had Emma seen him agitated or angry, thrown off balance or even confused or hesitant. Was he even capable of love?

"If ye dunno believe me," Maggie said, once again guessing Emma's thoughts correctly, "then watch him carefully and ye'll see. He canna help himself any more than ye and Finn." With a sigh, Maggie turned back to her branches, her nimble fingers arranging them beautifully as her gaze drifted to her sleeping children near the fire.

Too distracted by her encounter with Finn as well as Maggie's words, Emma mostly stood off to the side for the remainder of the evening, her fingers twirling a lone ribbon between them. While Maggie worked tirelessly, Emma did as she was bid and watched Cormag like a hawk, trying her best not to be too obvious.

At first, she did not notice anything that would prove Maggie's words right. Calm and collected, he spoke to Garrett, completely unaffected by the vibrant words that flew from his friend's mouth. Emma was about to abandon her observations when a muscle in his jaw twitched and his chest rose and fell with an utterly slow breath as though he was steeling himself for something.

Emma's eyes went wide and her gaze was drawn to the entrance where Moira just now stepped across the threshold. Tall and fair, she bore a striking contrast to Cormag's shadow-like appearance. Where he easily melted into the background, Moira stood out, drawing all eyes to her. And yet, while Cormag was always met with respect, the golden-haired outsider from Clan Brunwood was only ever shown distrust wherever she went. Emma wondered what was behind the whispers that circulated around Moira's banishment from her own clan.

Neither one of them looked at the other, and yet, it seemed utterly clear that they were very much aware of one another. Emma stared with wide eyes as Cormag continued his conversation with Garrett while Moira offered her help to Maggie. Both hid behind an outward appearance of disinterest whereas a dedicated observer could neither miss the fleeting looks cast in the other's direction nor the subtle ways they moved to keep each other in sight.

Shaking her head in utter disbelief, Emma stared at Cormag who drew in a sharp breath, all muscles in his body tensing, when Maggie accidentally knocked over a candle and it fell on Moira's sleeve. The young woman quickly pulled her arm back before its flame could touch the fabric of her dress and set it on fire.

Maggie apologised profusely while Moira kindly waved away her concern. A moment later, all was right again, and yet, Cormag still watched Moira like a hawk as though he feared for her even now.

Sinking down onto one of the benches near the hearth, Emma sighed, wondering if there was anyone in this world who was as aware of her as Cormag and Moira were of each other. Did Finn notice her the moment she walked into a room? Did his eyes linger when she was not looking? Was that what Maggie had been talking about? Was it truly something she, Emma, could not see because her own heart was involved?

Oh, if only she could be as certain about Finn as she now felt about Cormag and Moira.

After leaving Emma in the corridor, Finn went outside and wandered around in the cold, hoping the fresh air would clear his mind. Still, when he returned to the great hall an hour later, his body still felt as tense as a spring. While his heart ached to find Emma and continue what they had started, his mind wondered how *she* felt about it. Had he been the only one affected by their kiss? Had it been merely a pleasurable encounter for her? Or had it been as life-changing for her as it had been for him?

Walking around a corner, Finn bumped into Garrett, who had a pleased smile on his face and a bounce in his step. Lately, Garrett seemed utterly happy, and Finn could not deny that he envied him.

"Ye look awful," Garrett commented as his narrowed gaze swept over Finn. "I thought ye wanted to talk to the lass." His gaze darkened, and he pulled Finn to the side. "Did it not go well?"

Finn sighed, "I dunno know. I...We..."

"Out with it!"

Chuckling, Finn shook his head, feeling suddenly very self-conscious with his friend's watchful eyes on him. "I kissed her."

Garrett's face split into a large grin, and he clasped a companionable hand on Finn's shoulder. "About time!"

Finn's shoulders slumped as he began to pace. "But what now? We didn't have a chance to speak. I dunno know how she felt about it." Turning on his heel, he looked at Garrett. "All these past few years, we've," he scoffed, "all but hated each other. How are we-?"

"Nah!" Garrett boomed, a chuckle rumbling in his throat. "Ye didna hate each other. Ye've been in love all these years but managed to misunderstand each other."

The air rushed from Finn's lungs in one sharp *whoosh* as he heard Garrett utter these few simple words.

Garrett chuckled once more, "Ye didna know then?" he asked, his eyes twinkling with merriment as though Finn's torments were utterly laughable. "'Twas rather obvious."

"Was it?" Finn croaked, unable to deny the truth of Garrett's words. However, neither could he deny that it frightened him nearly witless. It was as though the world had turned upside down within a day, within a matter of moments. All he thought he knew was suddenly no more.

"Aye," Garrett confirmed, a hint of impatience coming to his gaze.

"And now ye need to decide what ye want. 'Tis a once in a lifetime chance at love, and ye'd be a fool to let it slip through yer fingers." He shrugged, a grin on his face. "But that's only my humble opinion."

Rubbing his hands over his face, Finn groaned. "I know. I know. 'Tis only that...that I keep wondering if 'tis truly love." Looking at Garrett, he sighed. "What if 'tis simply attraction? What if she doesna...?" Gritting his teeth, Finn cursed, wishing life could for once be simple and straightforward.

"She cares for ye," Garrett stated as though it were a fact. "She cares for ye as much as ye care for her."

Staring at his friend, Finn shrugged. "How do ye know?"

Exasperated, Garrett sighed. "Because ye dunno hate people ye're only mildly attracted to, ye hear me? Ye glared at her the way ye did because ye felt betrayed and ye canna feel betrayed if ye didna have hopes for more. There, 'tis all very simple."

"What about her?"

"She mightna have glared at ye, but the way she pretended not to see ye was quite telling if ye ask me." Taking a step forward, Garrett sighed. "If ye're truly not certain, then let her marry Vaughn and come to England with me."

Finn flinched, and only when Garrett's gaze dropped lower did he notice that his hands had balled into fists.

A triumphant grin came to Garrett's face. "But if that thought turns yer stomach, then 'tis safe to say that ye're in love."

"I didna know," Finn mumbled, remembering all those years when he had been so angry, running off to Clan MacKinnear because the mere sight of her was torment, reminding him daily that what his heart desired was never to be.

"Ye didna want to know," Garrett corrected, chuckling. "Listen, it came as quite the shock to me, too, when I first laid eyes on my wife." Inhaling a deep breath, he shook his head as though he still could not believe it. "It hit me in the chest like a hard punch. I was completely taken aback by the sudden intensity of my feelings for her. One moment, I didna even know she walked this earth, and in the next, I was in love. But now that I am, I canna wait to find her, to have her back in my arms and kiss her speechless."

Finn frowned at the wicked grin on his friend's face.

"She talks a lot," Garrett said by way of explaining. Then he sighed, and his face sobered. "Yer love is right here. Ye dunno have to go and search half of England for her, merely admit that ye're in love. Does that not sound simple?"

Finn had to admit that it did. Even though he could not be certain how Emma felt, he could finally admit to himself how *he* felt about *her*. And to his great shock, he realised that he was utterly in love with her.

If she was to marry anyone, it would be him!

Chapter Eight

LOUD & CLEAR

As the evening wore on, Emma settled deeper into her seat by the fireplace, only outwardly watching over Maggie's children. Inwardly, Emma was quite busy watching all those around her, suddenly taken with the desire to discover the subtle signs people could not suppress when they were near someone they cared about...or did not.

Not only Cormag seemed utterly incapable of leaving the great hall after finishing his conversation with Garrett, but Moira, too, lingered after all preparations for tomorrow's feast were finally taken care of and Maggie was satisfied.

At first glance, neither one of them drew anyone's attention as there were quite a few people seeking company after a long day. They stood in groups or sat around Maggie's newly-decorated tables, her watchful eyes ensuring that her decorations were not disturbed. Laughter and conversation echoed through the large hall, and the fire in the hearth lent it a warm feeling of safety and home.

As always, Moira sat by herself, and yet, from under her lashes she stole a glance at their tall, dark laird every now and then. Still, neither one seemed to be aware of the other's interest in them.

Emma shook her head, shocked by the human heart's inability to see clearly when its own welfare was concerned. Had she been this blind as well?

Of course, she had, and it had made her waste seven long years of her life!

Despite the almost magnetic connection between Cormag and Moira, they never dared look at one another, nor speak to the other, pretending they were nothing short of strangers. Emma felt oddly reminded of the past seven years and her attempts to meet Finn with polite indifference. Judging from Maggie's words, her friend had seen through her charade as easily as Emma could now see the truth about Cormag and Moira.

Turning her gaze toward her friend, Emma heaved a deep sigh when she saw Maggie speak to her husband. With hanging shoulders, Ian stood before her, his blue eyes dark, and yet, there was a silent plea in them that Emma had never noticed before. At some point, he reached out and brushed a tender hand over Maggie's arm. It was an achingly-sweet gesture, and yet, Maggie tensed.

Emma swallowed hard, her heart filling with pity when she saw the defeated look in Ian's eyes. Instantly, he took a step back as though his wife had slapped him.

"She does not love him," Emma mumbled under her breath, "but he loves her." Sadness engulfed her as she watched Maggie and Ian, for the first time noticing the distance that existed between them for what it was: longing. While Ian clearly longed for his wife, Maggie's heart was elsewhere. Something-or rather someone-stood between them. Once again, Emma wondered what had happened back in England before Maggie had come to Scotland. Had she left behind a great love? Had he died? Rejected her? If she had been in love, why on earth had she agreed to marry Ian?

Brushing a gentle hand over Blair's head when she stirred in her sleep, Emma sighed, reminding herself that love rarely made sense and was often driven by fear. Had she herself not been ready to accept Vaughn in order to protect her heart from being broken should Finn reject her?

Lifting her gaze, Emma spotted Vaughn standing across the hall, deep in conversation with his father. Still, his eyes occasionally travelled to her, and she saw kindness and interest there. He was a good man, and Emma had no doubt he would be a good husband to her. Still, what did she have to offer him in return?

Unlike Cormag, who had taken note of Moira's presence right away, Emma had not even noticed when Vaughn had stepped into the hall. How long had he stood there? Emma could not say. Her heart would never belong to him, just like Maggie's heart still belonged to the unknown Englishman of her past. Even after all these years, Ian did not stand a chance, doomed to a loveless marriage, forever jealous of a man he had never met.

Emma knew that if she were to accept Vaughn, she would make him miserable. If not today, then eventually, and she could not do that to him. He deserved better.

As though to prove her right, Finn stepped into the hall in that moment...

...and Emma's heart leapt as though it wished to break from her chest and rush to his side.

As though he were a part of her, she felt him near, and the look in his eyes spoke of more than interest or even affection. It reminded her of the day he had found her by the loch after her father's burial.

Inexplicably, her eyes were drawn to him, and the very sight of him made the breath catch in her throat. Her head spun, and yet, she felt deliriously happy.

Finn, too, seemed eager to seek her out. Gone was the hateful glare of the past years, replaced by a look that spoke of utter longing and devotion, emotions so overwhelming that he needed to take a deep breath to contain them.

Out of the corner of her eye, Emma noticed Vaughn starting toward her.

Swept up in the very sight of her, Finn tensed when he noticed Vaughn's attention drawn to the beautiful woman near the fire, her cheeks flushed with warmth and her brown eyes aglow like the embers in the hearth.

His heart banged against his rib cage in panic, and fear flooded his blood, quickly carried into every fibre of his body.

Beside him, Garrett chuckled, "I guess yer heart just spoke loud and clear."

Finn inhaled a deep breath, fighting the urge to delay Vaughn's progress across the room by all means necessary.

"Dunno stand here like a fool," Garrett hissed in a whisper. "Go and tell the lass how ye feel...before 'tis too late." Then his friend gave him a determined shove and sent him on his way.

Finn's feet moved on their own, his gaze incapable of looking anywhere but at Vaughn and Emma. The moment the other man reached her side, Finn groaned under his breath, wishing he had not hesitated. What were they talking about? Was Vaughn asking for her hand in this very moment?

Would that not be cruel irony? The moment Finn had finally worked up the nerve to address the woman he had loved for seven years was the very moment another stole her away?

Squinting his eyes, Finn watched them as Vaughn offered Emma his hand to help her to her feet. Then he smiled at her, slightly bowing his head before he spoke.

Finn could have screamed in frustration, his eyes glued to the young couple by the hearth, wishing and at the same time fearing to know what was being said.

Then Vaughn's face stilled, and Finn stopped in his tracks, his heart slamming to a halt as hope surged through his being.

More words were exchanged, and Finn reminded himself to put one foot in front of the other. He could not falter now.

"Pardon me," he said rather formally when he reached their side. His gaze met Vaughn's, dark and forlorn, and then turned to Emma, her own saddened as well. What had passed between them? "Emma, may I speak to ye for a moment."

Gritting his teeth, Vaughn inhaled a deep breath, and for a short moment, his gaze returned to Emma, a hint of incredulity in it. Then he mumbled something under his breath and stalked off.

When Finn turned to look at Emma, sadness as well as a hint of guilt clung to her face, and yet, there was something in her eyes that gave him hope. A smile seemed to tickle her lips, and the brown in her eyes shone deeper and warmer than he had ever seen it. "Can I speak to ye?"

This time, she did smile. "Aye," came her voice, light and breathy as though her own heart was racing as fast as his.

Breathing a sigh of relief, Finn took her by the elbow and guided her to the back of the hall and out into the corridor where they had kissed only a few hours ago. All the while, his heart thudded wildly in his chest, afraid to have been misled and be rejected by her.

Still, he needed to know if she cared for him or he would regret it for the rest of his life.

Chapter Nine

FOREVER IN A DAY

Emma's heart still ached for Vaughn, her inner eye unable to abandon the disappointed look on his face when she had stopped him before he could ask for her hand. He had looked so hopeful and eager, no apprehension in his heart with regard to her answer. Disappointment had come swift and mercilessly, and yet, the blue in his eyes had not spoken of a crushed heart. Had his regard for her truly been as deep as she had feared? Perhaps he would recover swiftly and would soon be able to grant his heart to a woman who could offer him hers in return.

Emma could only hope so.

The look on Finn's face when he had stepped up to her and Vaughn had been one of tense apprehension. Even now his hand on her elbow felt hardened by trepidation as he led her away.

Without looking at one another, they walked out into the corridor where he had found her earlier that evening, and Emma's breath caught in her throat at the memory of their encounter. Never in her life had she felt closer to anyone but in that moment. The way he had looked at her, spoken to her, the way he had said her name, his voice heavy with affection, and yet, vibrating with impatience, daring her to evade his question, had felt utterly wonderful as though they had always been close, kindred spirits, kept apart by circumstance. Did she dare believe it to be true?

Afraid of what he might say to her, and yet, wishing to hear him speak, Emma turned to Finn, noting the tension that held him almost rigid. Only a muscle in his jaw twitched, betraying an inner turmoil she would not have suspected. "Are ye all right?" she asked, trying to catch his gaze. "Ye look upset."

A scoff flew from his lips, and he shook his head. "Aye, I'm upset, lass." His voice sounded rough and filled with emotions held back. He inhaled a deep breath, and then his eyes met hers, held hers as though he did not dare look away. "Did Vaughn ask for yer hand?"

Emma flinched, and yet, her heart leapt into her throat with joy. "Well, he…," she began, noting the way his shoulders drew upward and his hands balled into fists. If she allowed herself to believe her own eyes, she would think he was jealous! Could that truly be?

A lot had happened in only one day. A lot had happened that Emma had not seen coming or would ever have expected. Still, she remembered the way he had spoken to her, the way he had looked at her-looked not glared! She remembered his kiss, speaking not merely of passion but affection, perhaps even love. She also remembered him asking her if she intended to marry Vaughn.

And now, here he was wanting to know-desperately from the looks of it!-if Vaughn had asked for her hand.

"What did ye say?" Finn growled out, and Emma could have sighed with happiness. He truly cared for her! All of a sudden, it was as plain as day. How could she not have seen it before?

"Emma!"

Jarred from her happy thoughts, Emma took note of the almost murderous expression in Finn's eyes as he glared at her. Still, this glare was a far-fetch from the one he had bestowed upon her at every encounter in the past seven years. It spoke less of anger and more of impatience, of a desperate need to have his question answered.

"Aye?" she said innocently, devilishly enjoying the pained look in his eyes.

"Would ye answer me?"

Cocking her head, she looked at him. "Why do ye wish to know?"

Finn's teeth ground together as he tried his best to keep himself under control. Still, Emma could see the pulse in his neck thudding wildly. His face darkened, and the steps that carried him toward her held something menacing. "Emma!" he warned once more as his steps urged her back against the wall.

Still, Emma could not help but smile. "If ye wish to know," she replied, lifting her chin as his hands settled to the left and right of her head, trapping her between himself and the wall, "then tell me why ye followed me that morning. Ye never answered me."

Finn's gaze narrowed, and a touch of incredulity came to his face. Inhaling a deep breath, he briefly closed his eyes. "I followed ye that morning because," he swallowed hard, "because yer kiss touched me... and I wanted to speak to ye."

A gust of air rushed from Emma's lungs, and her eyes suddenly misted with tears. "But...but ye said it hadna been a true kiss. Why then-?"

"It had been for me," he interrupted her, his gaze tracing the lone tear that rolled down her cheek, "but when I heard ye speak to yer friends, I knew it hadna been one for ye." His gaze met hers, and all of a sudden, she saw a different question there.

Once again, Emma felt like a young girl about to steal a kiss one cold wintry morning. She felt daring and adventurous. Her blood boiled in her veins, and her heart thudded loudly in her chest.

And then everything was simple.

As she had seven long years ago, Emma pulled Finn down into a kiss.

For a moment, he froze as he had then. Only this time, his paralysis lasted a mere second before his hands dropped from the wall and pulled her into his arms. He held her tightly and returned her kiss with the same longing she had felt in him when he had kissed her earlier that day.

Had only a few hours passed since then?

It felt like a lifetime.

Finn's heart danced and skipped and sang as he held the woman he loved in his arms.

Her kiss had caught him off guard as it had all those years ago. Only now, it was far from a soft peck of her lips on his, quick and rushed before she had darted away. Now, she lay in his arms as though she never wanted to leave again, her kiss demanding and an intention behind it that whispered of promises.

When she pulled back, her eyes shone bright and steady. "I kissed ye that day," she whispered, "because I wanted to."

"Aye?" was all Finn could articulate in that moment as he stared down at her, a part of him urging him not to believe his own eyes.

"Aye," she confirmed before her lips brushed against his once more.

Clearing his throat, Finn lifted his head, a frown drawing down his brows. "Then why the dare? Why did ye not simply-?"

"Simply?" Emma exclaimed, her eyes widening with annoyance as she shook her head at him. "There's nothing simple about...about declaring one's feelings." Lifting her chin in defiance, she glared up at him. "I might as well ask why ye didna confront me then and there. Why did ye never say anything in all those years?"

Finn's shoulders slumped when he saw the same fear in her eyes he had harboured in his own heart all this time. "I...I was afraid ye would reject me," he finally admitted, his heart clenching even now at the thought of showing himself so vulnerable. "I heard ye laugh and say our kiss was nothing, that it had meant nothing to ye. It broke my heart."

Emma sighed, and the anger vanished from her eyes. "I felt the same. I...I accepted the dare because it gave me an excuse to kiss ye without having it mean anything...if it didna mean anything to ye."

Shaking his head, Finn chuckled. "We were both trying to protect ourselves and ended up miserable for seven years. Can ye imagine what would've happened if I had reached ye that morning before ye could have met up with yer friends?"

A soft smile came to Emma's lips. "What would ye have done? Would ye have told me the truth?"

Finn shrugged. "I dunno know. I can only hope I would have said... or done something to show ye that yer kiss had meant something to me, that ye could trust me to confide in me as well."

"And then?" she asked, her eyes shining with hope.

Finn shrugged as his heart calmed and the fear of rejection slowly receded. Still, he remembered the way she had teased him, tortured him, in fact, she still had not answered his question about Vaughn's proposal. "I dunno know," he replied, willing the joy in his heart not to show on his face. "All I'm asking of ye now is to be honest with me. If ye dunno care for me, then tell me so honestly so that I might move on and find love elsewhere."

At his words, Emma blinked, shock coming to her brown eyes before her hands shot forward and she grabbed him by the front of his shirt. "Don't ye dare! Ye're mine, Finnegan MacDrummond. D'ye hear? Ye're mine, and ye've always been." She inhaled a deep breath, the look in her eyes fierce as she held on to him. "I only wish I'd claimed ye earlier."

Finn's heart danced in his chest as it had never before. "Claim me?" he asked with a chuckle as his arms came around her, holding her to him with the same determination he saw in her eyes as well. "Are ye claiming me now?"

A wicked smile came to her face. "Aye, I am."

"And I have no say in the matter?"

Shaking her head, she pulled him down to her until their noses almost touched. "I'm afraid not." Then she kissed him the way she had kissed him only moments ago, and Finn finally realised that her heart truly belonged to him.

"Does that mean ye're not going to marry Vaughn?" he asked teasingly. Still, his heart tensed at the mere thought of her tied to another. After all, marriages were agreed upon for all kinds of reasons. Simply because she did not love Vaughn did not mean she had not agreed to marry him.

Frowning, she stared at him. "Of course not. It wouldna be fair to him. He deserves better."

Finn chuckled, enjoying the feel of her in his arms. "And I don't?"

"No, ye and I were made for each other," she said as though stating a fact. Finn had to admit it rather pleased him. "We're both equally fearful and stubborn to have not said a word about this for seven years." For a moment, she shook her head in disbelief, a hint of disappointment on her face. Then, however, her gaze met his, and her eyes lit up with happiness. "We deserve each other, wouldn't ye agree?"

"Aye," Finn laughed, realising that he could not wait to get to know the woman he had loved for so long. Never had they truly spoken to one another, and yet, he had never felt closer to anyone before.

Pulling her tighter against him, Finn looked down at her, feeling at peace for the first time in years. "We should've been together all those years," he whispered, "but there's no use in crying over something we canna change. All we can do is make certain that we willna waste any more time."

Smiling up at him, Emma nodded.

Finn swallowed, then inhaled a deep breath before he said, "Emma Stewart, will ye marry me...tomorrow?"

Her brown eyes went wide. "Tomorrow? But 'tis Christmas!"

"I dunno care," Finn said laughing. "I dunno want to waste another minute. I want ye to be my wife, and I want to start our lives together...tomorrow, and not a moment later."

Laughing, Emma flung herself into his arms. "Aye, I'll marry ye...tomorrow."

With his heart overflowing with joy, Finn spun his bride-to-be in a circle, holding her tight as they hugged and laughed, both overwhelmed by all that could happen in a day.

Finn vowed that he would never again allow fear to hold him back.

It was not worth it.

Not for a single moment.

Epilogue

Never would Emma have imagined that she had in fact decorated the great hall the day before for her own wedding day. And yet, here she was, dressed in her finest gown, a smile on her face she could not seem to shake and a man by her side whom she had loved for as long as she could remember.

After Finn had asked for her hand the night before, they had immediately gone to seek out Cormag to ask for his blessing as well as his approval to have their wedding ceremony on Christmas morning. Oddly enough, Cormag had acted as though he had all but expected them.

And he had not been the only one.

The whole of Clan MacDrummond gathered in the great hall that morning, their eyes shining with joy and their cheeks flushed from the cold. Cheerful whispers echoed through the hall until the moment the wedding ceremony began. Then silence fell over them as everyone strained to hear Emma and Finn exchange their vows.

While *everyone* had been surprised that Emma and Finn were to be married on Christmas morning, *no one* had been surprised to hear that they *were* to be married. In fact, many had congratulated them, mumbling something about them finally getting their happy ending. It would seem the whole of Clan MacDrummond had been aware of Emma's and Finn's true feelings for one another and had considered it only a matter of time until they would tie the knot.

The only ones who had been blind had been Emma and Finn themselves.

Smiling at Finn as he held her hand in his, Emma pushed all thoughts of the past away. Certainly, they had wasted time, being so fearful of rejection, of having their hearts broken. However, dwelling on that loss would only cost them more.

Today was a day for celebration in every way, and tomorrow, their new life would begin.

Emma could not wait. She only wished that others would find the same happiness that had so unexpectedly found her. Was there still a chance for Maggie and Ian to find joy in their marriage? Would Cormag and Moira ever admit that they were in love? Would Garrett find his wife and bring her back to Seann Dachaigh Tower?

Emma could only hope so.

After all, a lot could happen in a day.

THE END

Thank you for reading *Dared & Kissed*!

Moira's and Cormag's story is waiting for you in *Banished & Welcomed – The Laird's Reckless Wife*. We will learn more about Moira as she tries to find her place among the MacDrummonds and finds herself inexplicably drawn to their taciturn laird, Cormag MacDrummond.

Read a Sneak-peek

Banished & Welcomed
The Laird's Reckless Wife
(#3 Highland Tales)

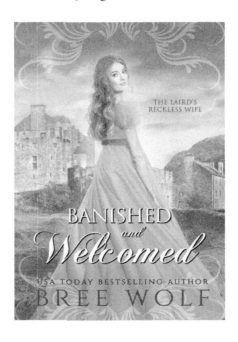

Prologue

GREYSTONE CASTLE, SCOTTISH HIGHLANDS, AUTUMN
1806 (OR A VARIATION THEREOF)

TWO YEARS EARLIER

The key turning in the lock sent a deafening sound through the small
chamber, a chamber that had been hers for as long as she could
remember. Never had it been a prison cell though.

Never.

But that had changed the day Moira Brunwood, once a proud
daughter of Clan Brunwood, had betrayed her own kin.

Swallowing, Moira rose from the chair she had occupied for the
past hour, her gaze directed out at the land she loved, but would be
forced to leave that very day. Her hands brushed over her gown,
suddenly obsessed with smoothing out even the smallest wrinkle as she
turned toward the door.

Slowly, it swung open, revealing the tall stature of Alastair Brunwood, Moira's brother. His features were hard as his blue eyes settled
on her, anger burning in their depth as she had never seen before. His
lips were pressed into a thin line, and the muscles in his neck were

rigid as he jerked his head toward her. "Come," he all but growled, his voice harsh, revealing how deep her betrayal had cut him.

Still, Moira rejoiced at that single word for it was the first one she had heard him utter in many weeks. Or had it only been days? Moira could not say. Time had lost all meaning as she had been locked away, her heart and mind retreating from the world, from what she had done. How often had she sat in this chair, staring out at the land that was no longer hers?

She would never know.

And it did not matter, did it?

Her hands trembled as Moira stepped forward. She could feel tears stinging the backs of her eyes, and yet, she did not dare look away for this was her last day.

Her last day at Greystone Castle.

Her last day with her clan.

With her brother.

Bracing herself, Moira drew closer to where Alastair stood, her heart twisting painfully at the sight of his taut face. The way his eyes refused to meet hers almost brought her to her knees, and in that moment, all she wanted was to sink down and weep for the mistakes she had made, the illusions she had entertained. How had she not seen this coming? How could she have been so wrong?

Brushing a blond strand behind his right ear, Alastair stepped from the room, waiting for her to follow. He stood like a sentinel, eyes directed forward as though he did not even see her.

Or did not wish to.

For the first time in weeks, Moira stepped out into the corridor, the grey stones of the walls surrounding her as familiar to her as the back of her hand. Her whole life had taken place in this castle, and now it would have no place in her future. It was hard to believe, and a part of Moira felt as though this was no more than one of her dreams.

Dreams that showed her things that were not real but could be one day. They had been her downfall, and not a day passed that she did not curse the Fates for allowing her glimpses of a future that would now never be hers.

With her head bowed, Moira followed her brother down the back staircase. The day was still young, and only a dim glow of the autumn's light reached inside the thick stone walls. A chill crawled up her arms, and she drew her shawl more tightly around herself.

All was silent as they stepped out into the courtyard and turned toward the stables. Fog lingered all around her, shrouding everything in a thick blanket, and the air smelled faintly of salt, whispering of the sea nearby.

Her eyes swept over the familiar courtyard where they had danced not too long ago, celebrating their laird's happy marriage.

Connor's marriage to an English lady.

With her lips pressed into a thin line, Moira picked up her step and hurried after her brother. Not even now could she think of Henrietta Brunwood, Connor's wife, without feeling a stab to the heart. After all, it had been the slender, pale Englishwoman who had brought about Moira's downfall. She had bewitched Connor, stolen his heart as well as his hand, so that he had no longer been able to see Moira.

A lone tear escaped and rolled down her cheek as Moira quickly reached up and brushed it away. There was no point in falling to pieces now. She had cried all the tears she had possessed for the loss of her future.

The future she had seen in her dreams.

The future she had been promised.

And although it was lost to her now, her dreams still stayed with her as though to taunt her.

Every now and then when sleep took her, she would travel to the moment that had urged her to act, to conspire against Henrietta, the moment that had led her down a path of betrayal.

Again, she would see herself standing atop a lush green hill, Connor by her side, his arm wrapped around her shoulders as her head rested against his strong chest. Together, they gazed across the land, their eyes sweeping over the men and women and children of their clan, preparing for the Highland Games. Moira could see the Brunwood banner flapping in the strong breeze, and a smile would come to her lips.

Again, and again, she had seen this in her dreams. Dreams she knew to be a whisper of the future. It was a gift she had had since she had been a wee lass. A gift of the Old Ones. A gift she was to use to secure her clan's future.

And so, Moira had acted.

She had taken steps to rid her cousin Connor of his new English wife, believing - no, knowing! -that *she* -Moira- was meant to lead their clan by his side, not Henrietta. After all, her dreams had told her so, and never once had her dreams been wrong.

Until now.

Stepping into the stables, Moira breathed in the warmth of the animals mingling with the strong scent of hay and manure. She watched her brother lead two horses from their boxes, their saddles in place and a few belongings tied behind them.

Alastair kept his gaze firmly fixed on the task at hand, never once even glancing in her direction. He was a seasoned hunter, trained in combat, and had the instincts of a warrior. He knew without looking where she was and what she was doing. He always had, and Moira had always felt special because of it.

She was his little sister, and he was her big brother.

At least, they had been.

Once.

"Goodbye, Moira."

Spinning around, Moira stared at Connor standing only a few feet behind her, his bear-like stature blocking the door. He was tall and broad, but he moved with the same ease and precision as Alastair. His black hair and full beard gave him a somewhat darker countenance; however, Moira knew that Connor was a man full of laughter and mirth.

Only now, his eyes were hard, and his lips pressed into a thin line as he regarded her with the same sense of disbelief and disappointment she had seen in his gaze since he had learnt of her betrayal. Since he had realised that *she* had been the one to almost cost him his life. That *she* had been the one to threaten his wife.

A wife he loved with all his heart and soul.

Moira knew that now, but she had not known it then.

To her great dismay, fresh tears shot to her eyes, and she clenched her teeth, willing them to not show themselves. After all that had happened, all Moira had left was a small bit of pride, and she would fight to keep it. "I'm sorry," she said nonetheless; her voice, however, was even and free of the deep regret she felt. "I swear I never meant for ye to be hurt...or her." She swallowed. "I didna know what he had planned. I swear it."

Swallowing, Connor nodded. His gaze momentarily slid to Alastair standing somewhere behind her, tending to the horses, before he drew closer, his dark eyes fixed on her face as though he hoped to read her thoughts. "I believe ye, Lass, as Old Angus made no secret of how he used ye for his cause."

Moira drew in a shuddering breath at the memory of the hateful, old man who had seen Connor's English wife as a threat to the clan, a threat that needed to be eliminated. He had gathered men and led them in an attack against Connor, thinking him weak for allowing the British to infiltrate their home.

And to her shame, Moira had believed his lies and aided him in his quest.

In the end, it had been Henrietta's courage and Alastair's loyalty that had saved Connor's life. Moira still felt sick at the thought of how close he had come to dying that day.

And she would have been responsible.

"But ye betrayed me," Connor told her. "Ye betrayed all of us. I understand how Angus could have done what he did." He shook his head. "After the horrors of Culloden, he hasna been right in the head. But ye?"

Moira nodded. "I know. I canna believe it myself. All I can do now is apologise."

"And make amends," Connor told her, his eyes hard as they held hers. "Yer past is sealed. It canna be changed, but ye're still the master of yer future." Taking a step closer, he placed a hand on her shoulder. "I know ye've been misled and that ye're sorry, but that isna enough. Ye need to find a way to lead a good life." He sighed, "Ye know ye canna stay here."

Swallowing, Moira nodded.

Connor glanced over her shoulder, his eyes no doubt meeting Alastair's before he looked down at her once more. "For yer brother's sake,

I give ye this chance. Use it wisely for it shall be yer last." Then he took a step back, and his hand slid from her shoulder. "Goodbye, Moira. May yer dreams not lead ye astray again." Then he turned and walked away, severing the bond that had connected them since childhood. Their lives would now lead them down different paths, and Moira wondered if she would ever see him again.

As she followed Alastair out of the courtyard, feeling her mare's strong flanks beneath her legs, Moira drew in a deep breath. Her body shuddered with the weight of the moment that was finally upon her, a moment she had dreaded for the past weeks, and her eyes filled with tears.

And this time, she let them fall for her heart broke anew as they rode out of Greystone Castle, leaving behind a life, a family, a home.

Outcast.

Banished.

Exiled.

All these terms that had been coursing around in her mind these past few weeks spoke to one deep-seated fear: loneliness. Now, Moira was alone in the world with no one to care whether she lived or died. She would live among strangers, strangers who would no doubt look upon her with disgust and mistrust for her deeds had spread throughout the lands, even reaching the ears of those far away.

And Moira could not blame them. She had no defence, no justification, no excuse or explanation. Aye, she had been misled; still, the decision had been hers.

She had failed them as well as herself.

Glancing over her shoulder, Moira watched Greystone Castle vanish a little more with each step their horses surged forward, a heavy fog settling around its walls and upon its towers. It was as though the Old Ones, too, were punishing her, hiding those she loved from her view.

Always had Moira had the Sight, and now, she could not see.

Days passed in silence as they travelled onward across the land, and Moira's heart grew heavier. Her limbs felt weak, and it was a struggle to pull herself into the saddle each morning. Her mind was numb, clouded with guilt and fear as well as another moment of loss she knew would come.

When they spotted *Seann Dachaigh* Tower, home of Clan MacDrummond, around midday on their fifth day since leaving Greystone Castle, Moira felt an icy fist grab her heart and squeeze it mercilessly. She shivered against the cold that swept through her body, gritting her teeth as she fought for control.

Without so much as glancing in her direction, Alastair spurred on his horse as though he could not wait to rid himself of her. Her betrayal had indeed cut deep, and Moira tried to gain comfort from the fact that his hatred of her would not be so profound if he had not loved her as much as she loved him.

Seann Dachaigh Tower, home of their mother's clan, was situated on a small rise, surrounded by Scotland's rolling hills as well as a small village. Its grey stone walls stood strong, surrounding a fortified inner castle, with only a large front gate to grant entrance. To Moira, it looked like a prison from whence there would be no escape, and her breath caught in her throat when despair washed over her in a powerful, suffocating wave.

Birds called overhead, and the scent of pine and hazel trees drifted through the air. The breeze tugged on Moira's blond tresses and brushed over her chilled skin raising goose bumps. Still, the mild hint of salt she detected brought her a small comfort, a reminder of home. The sky shone in a light blue, but Moira spotted dark clouds on the horizon.

A bad omen?

Wishing she could simply turn her mare around and ride away in the opposite direction, Moira paused atop a small slope, her blue eyes gazing down across the valley at the imposing structure that would be her home henceforth. Her fingers tightened on the reins, and she could feel her mare's agitation as she no doubt picked up on the unease that coursed through Moira's veins.

Noting her delay, Alastair pulled up his reins and turned his gelding around, thundering toward her. His eyes narrowed into slits, and a snarl curled up the corners of his mouth. "Ye willna dishonour this family further," he growled. "I willna allow it, do ye hear?"

Swallowing the lump in her throat, Moira nodded, then urged her mare onward, her gaze distant as she did not dare look at her brother. Was this how they were to part? Was this how she was to remember him?

When they finally reached the old structure, entering through the wide-open gate into the bustling courtyard, Alastair pulled up short and addressed a man carrying a bag of grain on his shoulder. A few words were exchanged before the man pointed him toward a small group of women standing near a well, chatting animatedly.

Moira dismounted; her fingers tightly curled around her mare's reins as she glanced around the inner courtyard. Eyes watched her, narrowed and full of suspicion. She heard whispers and felt stares digging into the back of her skull.

They knew.

They knew of her. They knew her story.

They had known she would come.

And they did not like her.

In fact, they loathed her and wished her gone.

With all her heart, Moira wished she could do as they desired, but her hands were tied. In this, she had no choice.

Turning her head, Moira saw her brother striding back toward her, an older woman by his side. Her light brown hair had streaks of grey, and her face looked stern as her blue eyes swept over Moira in displeasure.

Stopping in front of her, Alastair turned to the woman by his side. "This is Aunt Fiona. She's agreed to give ye shelter." The tone in Alastair's voice rang with disapproval, and he looked at their late mother's older sister with a hint of apology as though he loathed burdening her with his dishonourable sister.

Fiona gave her a sharp nod. "I warn ye, Lass. Folks do not look kindly on those who betray their own kin. I suggest ye do as ye're told and keep yer head down." She sighed, her blue eyes gliding over Moira's appearance, the niece she had not seen since she had been a wee bairn. "But first, ye'll meet the laird." She turned to go. "Come."

Moira's heart thudded to a halt when she turned back to look at her brother, only to see him walking away. In a few strides, he had crossed to where he had left his gelding, taken up the reins and swung himself into the saddle.

Panic swept through Moira as she stared at him. Her lower lip trembled, and tears ran freely down her face. Would he not even say goodbye to her?

Alastair's face looked stoic as he stared straight ahead, eyes focused on the large opening in the wall. The muscles in his jaw tensed, and he kicked his horse's flanks with more vigour than necessary. The gelding surged forward, shaking its large head, no doubt confused about his master's unkind treatment.

Look at me! Moira pleaded silently as she watched her brother ride away. *Please, look at me!*

But he did not.

He rode on stoically.

Moira's breath came fast as her vision began to blur before her eyes. Her knees buckled, and she groped blindly for something to hold on to, something to keep her upright as the world began to spin, threatening to throw her off her feet.

"Ye canna blame him, Lass," Fiona grumbled beside her as she grasped Moira's hands, pulling her around to face her. "He's a proud man, and he loved ye dearly." Fiona shook her head, her blue eyes sharp as she watched her niece. "Nay, ye canna blame him. He needs time. A lot of time. Perhaps more than he has." Then she turned toward the castle's keep pulling Moira with her.

Together, they crossed the courtyard, climbed the steps to the large oak door and then entered the great hall.

Moira saw very little of her surroundings as her heart ached within her chest. With each step she took, she had to fight the urge to sink to her knees as tears continued to stream down her face.

"Pull yourself together, Lass," her aunt reprimanded her as she guided their feet down a long corridor that seemed to go on forever, leading them far away from the loud hustle bustle in the great hall. "Our laird is a kind man, but he willna take kindly to those who only weep for themselves." She scoffed. "I dunno why he granted ye sanc-tuary when yer laird sent word of what ye'd done. Many argued against it, but he has a way of knowing things others do not." Her aunt stopped, fixing Moira with her sharp blue eyes. "Dunna make him regret this small mercy, do ye hear me, Lass?"

Moira could only nod as she wiped the tears from her eyes, suddenly overwhelmed by the thought that strangers would see her in this state of despair. Of course, she could not expect compassion, sympathy or even pity.

And yet, her heart ached for it.

On they continued down the corridor until they came to a lone door at the very end of it. There, Fiona stopped and lifted a hand to knock.

"Come in."

The laird's voice rang strong and commanding, but not unkind, and Moira wondered what kind of man he was. Clearly, he was held in high esteem by the people of his clan, and she had only ever heard Connor speak with great respect of Cormag MacDrummond.

Their clans had been close long ago but had drifted apart since Culloden and the destruction of the Highland clans. The years had been tough, and trust had been hard to come by. What would it be like to live among another clan as one who had betrayed her own kin? Would they lock her in her chamber as well? Afraid she would betray them, too?

Moira swallowed, and a cold chill ran down her back as she followed her aunt into the laird's study.

Large with narrow windows, it was a simple room that held only the laird's desk as well as a couple of chairs and cabinets. It was not designed for comfort, but for practicality, for handling the clan's affairs.

Now, she too was a clan affair.

Straightening, Moira lifted her head, determined not to cower. As much as she felt like sinking to the ground, she would not give the MacDrummond laird the satisfaction. She would stand tall with her head held high. Aye, she would apologise and voice her regrets-as she had so many times before. She would accept the blame as it was rightfully hers. However, she would not allow him to frighten her, to force her to hide the pride that had always lived in her chest.

After all, she was of Clan Brunwood, a proud Highland clan, and even if her legs trembled with fear and her heart ached with loneliness, she would rather die than reveal her inner turmoil to a man who would no doubt look down on her with suspicion for the rest of her life.

As Moira followed her aunt and came to stand in front of the laird's large desk, her eyes swept over his tall stature as he stood with his back to her, staring at the wall for all she knew. He was a large man with broad shoulders and raven-black hair, and for a thoroughly terrifying moment, he reminded Moira of Connor. Would her past haunt her wherever she went?

Perhaps she deserved it.

"I present to ye my niece," her aunt spoke into the silence of the room, "Moira Brunwood. Her brother delivered her to me only moments ago."

Moira glanced at her aunt, wondering about the need to explain what she heard in the older woman's voice. Was Fiona afraid the laird would fault her somehow? Was she doing what she could to distance herself from her traitorous niece?

Moira sighed knowing she could not blame her aunt for what she did. Aye, it would have been nice to have someone on her side; however, she had to admit that she had not once thought about what her presence here at *Seann Dachaigh* Tower would mean for her aunt. How would it affect Fiona's life? How would people treat her? Look upon her?

The laird's broad shoulders rose and fell as he inhaled a long breath. Then he slowly turned around as though apprehensive to look upon her.

Moira gritted her teeth, feeling a surge of anger rise in her heart. Why on earth had he agreed to Connor's request if he did not want her here? Why would he-?

The breath caught in Moira's throat the moment Cormag MacDrummond's charcoal grey eyes met hers. Of all the things she had expected to feel in that moment-shame, regret, guilt, even fear-she was completely unprepared for the sudden jolt that seemed to stop her heart and make it come alive at the same time. Warmth streamed into her chest as though the sun had risen after a long absence, and she felt the corners of her lips curl upward, unable to contain the exhilaration that had claimed her so unexpectedly.

Overwhelmed, Moira clasped her hands together, needing something to hold onto.

Never had she felt like this before.

Not even Connor had ever inspired such...such...

In that moment, Moira finally realised that she had never been in love with Connor Brunwood.

Series Overview

LOVE'S SECOND CHANCE: TALES OF LORDS & LADIES

LOVE'S SECOND CHANCE: TALES OF DAMSELS & KNIGHTS

LOVE'S SECOND CHANCE: HIGHLAND TALES

FORBIDDEN LOVE SERIES

HAPPY EVER REGENCY SERIES

THE WHICKERTONS IN LOVE

For more information visit www.breewolf.com

About Bree

USA Today bestselling and award-winning author, Bree Wolf has always been a language enthusiast (though not a grammarian!) and is rarely found without a book in her hand or her fingers glued to a keyboard. Trying to find her way, she has taught English as a second language, traveled abroad and worked at a translation agency as well as a law firm in Ireland. She also spent loooong years obtaining a BA in English and Education and an MA in Specialized Translation while wishing she could simply be a writer. Although there is nothing simple about being a writer, her dreams have finally come true.

"A big thanks to my fairy godmother!"

Currently, Bree has found her new home in the historical romance genre, writing Regency novels and novellas. Enjoying the mix of fact and fiction, she occasionally feels like a puppet master (or mistress? Although that sounds weird!), forcing her characters into ever-new situations that will put their strength, their beliefs, their love to the test, hoping that in the end they will triumph and get the happily-ever-after we are all looking for.

If you're an avid reader, sign up for Bree's newsletter on www. breewolf.com as she has the tendency to simply give books away. Find out about freebies, giveaways as well as occasional advance reader copies and read before the book is even on the shelves!

Connect with Bree and stay up-to-date on new releases: